The Calumnist Malefesto
And Other Improbable Yarns

Benoit Chartier
Aug 30th 2018

BENOIT CHARTIER

Cover Design by: Cory Tibbits
Copyright © 2013 Benoit Chartier
All rights reserved.

ISBN:1482333465
ISBN 13:9781482333466

Library of Congress Control Number: 2013902231
CreateSpace Independent Publishing Platform
North Charleston, South Carolina

I would like to dedicate this book to Mariko and Kota, the loves of my life. Without you, these stories would still be kicking around in my head, and not on the pages.

The Calumnist Malefesto

The floorboards groaned ominously underfoot as he walked slowly among the rows of stacked books. The shelves overflowed with all sorts of reading materials, from different eras, on all imaginable subjects. The ancient wooden libraries loomed heavily, almost menacingly, above him, daring him to approach. He had walked into the old store with no particular goal in mind but was impressed by the sheer amount of books, magazines, as well as odds and ends that surrounded him. The bookstore was located in what must have been an old department store that had been built at the turn of the century. The ceilings were ornately decorated, if dilapidated, a testimony to their former glory. The midday sun shone through the dirty front window, and in its rays danced lazy dust motes. A soft and eerie music wafted from an unseen radio somewhere near the counter, and the smell of age hung heavily in the air. There did not seem to be any kind of order to what the French would call a "capharnaum" of the slim alleys through which he carefully trod. There were piles of dusty books, from the creaking wooden floors, up to his armpits. He tried to navigate each tottering tower as best he could when his curiosity was attracted to the dark, crimson spine of a book on a low shelf, between two of these shaky stacks.

He carefully pulled on one of the piles until he was able to reach in and slowly remove the book from its hiding place. He looked at it appreciatively; the thick red binding was still solid, the aged yellow paper still sharp cornered. He blew the thin coat of dust that had settled on top away, creating a small storm in the process. The age of this book was great, and the crinkling of the pages as he turned them let off a waft of the ancient glues that held it together. He inhaled deeply, his mind reeling. Its sheer weight, and the possibilities it held, enthralled him. He was suddenly jerked back to reality when he heard a voice behind him.

"What is it?" asked the young girl, as she attempted to peer over his elbow at the treasure he held.

"This," he said somberly, "is *The Calumnist Malefesto*. The most unholy of unholies."

She stared at him, wide-eyed and disbelieving.

"It holds within it the secrets of creation and was damned by the ancient Gods themselves. The Elder Mages of the Orient poured all their secret knowledge into one maligned tome. Thousands of people were burned at the stake for practicing its Satanic rituals, for it contained forbidden knowledge that revealed what was supposed to be kept secret and out of the hands of men for all time. No magic can harm it; no spell can destroy it; no incantation can even singe it. Such is the strength of the power it holds. It knows no master and bows to no one. It will share the wisdom of its power only with those who denounce all other dark arts and pledge their hearts to its rule. The officials of the Church say that the Devil himself and all his council worked tirelessly until they were able to break into the Garden of Eden to corrupt Adam and Eve with the seeds of what it held, causing their and all of humanity's down-fall. Alchemists of every age of man have attempted to break its code and make its contents known for their own twisted purposes, but to no avail. For thousands of years, it was kept hidden from all, its perfidious and evil influence the greatest fear of all religious institutions. Secret societies were forced to hide it during the persecutions. Some claimed that its ink was made with the collected tears of a million tortured angels; that its pages were the tanned, flayed skins of forty of the most depraved demons to have walked the earth after their fall from grace. This page marker may be one of the quills of the demon Abaddon, the Guardian of the Pit of Hell, stolen from him as he slept. There is more concentrated denial of anything that is holy within this book than Lucifer ever could conjure within his dark heart in all of eternity, but I am sure he still tries. The Papal See was responsible for the banning of this execrable work, of the burning, of the torture of anyone who knew anything even remotely related to it. The *Necronomicon*, by the 'Mad Arab' Abdul Alhazred, one of the other most traitorous books ever spawned, is considered a children's tale and a work of pure fiction in comparison. No one has yet to uncover all of the *Malefesto*'s secrets, the depth of its twisted knowledge being incomprehensible to human minds. The forces of all those who want to keep us blissfully ignorant of the damage it can cause still work today toward its suppression. Yet here it is. It somehow escaped its captors. It probably ensnared the soul of one of its jailors in the secret libraries of the Vatican and was able to make its getaway. I can feel the power it emanates even now, coursing through my hands. *The Calumnist Malefesto*, the 'Liars' Damned Handbook' — it is mine!" He leered at the young girl, an evil grin plastered across his features, his tongue licking his lips lasciviously.

"That's just an old physics book. You're a dork, Brian," the young girl said, unimpressed, after having peered at its contents, and stalked off, pouting. After having thumbed through the pages filled with equations, Brian quietly returned the book to the shelf, snorted a giggle, and walked away.

A Visit from Mr. Dank

He lived in the small house at the end of a quiet street, next to the disused train tracks. Even though the house itself was old, it was well kept and in simple taste, in accordance with its owners' sensibilities. He was ancient and wise, and was almost done waiting. Summer had come and gone; fall was signaling retreat; and a single snowfall a few days earlier had made him decide to wait no longer. The pendulum of the grandfather clock in the sitting room swayed this way and that, steady as a heartbeat. It indicated that the hour was now four in the afternoon. In this part of the world, the sun was setting.

He sat in his rocking chair by the fireplace, the bright flames illuminating his gentle face. From the box in his hand he took a single white candle and straightened the wick with the tips of his fingers. He leaned somewhat creakily toward the fire, candle extended, and lit it. He retrieved the candle holder from the mantle and deposited a few drops of wax on to its base before wedging the candle gently into it, ensuring that it would not fall over. He went to the window and placed it on the windowsill, next to a carved wooden figurine of a sleeping kitten. His footsteps were muffled in his favorite slippers as he glided over the flowery carpet. He looked at the kitten and picked it up, staring at the letters that were carved into its base. He returned it to its place next to the candle and walked to the kitchen.

He picked up his knit sweater from the entrance and slipped it on first, the kitchen being quite drafty this time of year. He turned on the light and lit his gas stove. Then he took the kettle and filled it with water, careful not to spill it. He set it on the fire and went to the right-hand cupboard, where he picked a nice ginger-and-lemon tea. He considered Rooibos tea for a moment but set it down, content with his first choice. He placed the teabag inside a metal teabag holder then placed this inside his best teapot, set it on the counter on an ornate platter he had bought years ago, and chose two appropriate teacups for the occasion. He himself was partial to Japanese teacups, for their weight and how they retained heat so well when filled with a pungent green tea. This time, though, he selected two English cups (which his mother always had called "lady cups"), finding them more suitable for the circumstances. They were both delicate bone china, with gold-leaf decoration around the rims and vines in relief along the sides. These he placed on the tray on their matching saucers. He took two small silver spoons and placed them on the saucers. Then he opened the cupboard above his head and removed the honey container and placed it on the tray. He went to the refrigerator and took out the milk carton, filled a cream dispenser, then placed it on the tray as well.

As he did, he heard the expected knocking at the front door. He looked at the candle in his living room and noticed that in the darkness outside a gentle snow had begun to fall. He smiled and walked to the front door, turned on the porch light, and opened it to greet a gentleman in a long dark coat who smiled gently as he stood on the doorstep. The snow was gathering around his shoulders, but this did not seem to bother him at all.

"Hello, sir," the elderly gentleman said to his visitor, bowing.

"Hello to you, kind sir," said the visitor, bowing in return. "May I come in?"

"Of course! Of course! Where are my manners?" the older man exclaimed with consternation. He retreated to the interior of the house as he let the dignified-looking gentleman into his cloakroom. He offered to take the man's coat, and the gentleman removed it, handing it to him. He hung it up in the closet with care.

"May I interest you in some hot tea on this cold day?" he asked with deference.

"I would be rude to refuse, would I not?" replied the man, with a glint of humor in his eyes. "I'm sure you have prepared something for me in advance."

"I guess I shouldn't be surprised at your knowledge of things to come," the old man answered.

He invited his guest to come into his living room, where he could sit in the seat opposite his rocking chair. He went to the kitchen and turned off the stove, as the kettle had begun to whistle. He poured it steadily into the teapot, placed the lid back on, and covered it with a lovely blue knit tea cozy. He took the black-lacquered tea tray to the living room and placed it on the small round table between himself and his guest.

He sat down in his rocking chair and observed the smiling man before him with closer scrutiny for the first time since his arrival. He looked to be, he believed, in his mid-forties, with black hair, elegantly trimmed and arranged, with a slight curl at the ends. He had fine features, and his eyes crinkled a bit as he smiled. He wore a double-breasted black suit, with a beautiful cut he had never seen before. In his hands he held his black leather gloves. He wore leather shoes that went from black at the tips to dark-red at the heels. He had on an exquisite silk tie with this same color gradation, going from black at the neck to crimson toward the bottom. His shirt was an immaculate cream white, and his tie made a stark contrast upon it.

"What should I call you?" the old man asked, picking up the teapot and pouring it into the gentleman's cup as he held the lid.

"I have no preference really," came the reply. "You can call me Mr. Dark, if you like." He spoke with the quiet confidence of a being that never had known fear and never would.

"You seem like such a nice person," the old man said. "I don't understand why people are so terrified of you." He poured himself a cup as well, and the smell of lemon and ginger filled the air. He offered honey, which the man accepted, and milk, which he turned down.

"People mostly fear the things they do not understand, as you know. I always find it refreshing to have a conversation with someone who invites me into his home. Most are usually cowering in terror, pleading for their lives, trying to offer bargains I have no authority to accept, or trying to trick me somehow," Mr. Dark said, serious for a moment, as he held his cup of hot tea and took a short sip. He lifted his gaze to the elderly man, who was nodding, his brow furrowed. Then his features returned to his previous light-hearted smile.

"To be honest, I did not expect you to look this way," the old man said.

"I'm assuming you mean I should have come as a grinning angel of death, skeletal and dressed in a cowl, carrying a sickle, etcetera, etcetera, etcetera? I can certainly comprehend why humanity may have believed me to be this uncaring harbinger of doom in the past. I was very busy during the Middle Ages when that likeness of me was created. After all, plagues were rampaging through Europe at the time. Two-thirds of the population was decimated. You have no idea the overtime I had to pull. I'm still waiting for a vacation. No rest for the wicked, they say." He sighed, thinking back. "You have to remember, though, my friend, that no one ever has seen me and *lived* to tell about it. I've always been this way. It's human fear that makes me an abomination. It does make my job a bit more difficult, but not by much. I generally appear as one expects me to," he said, smiling at his host.

"You are not a deity, though, are you?" asked the older man, with curiosity.

"In certain cultures I am. It changes nothing in regard to my essence. I am merely an aspect of nature, and therefore, by extension, reality. I am part of a process. I allow for the birth and rebirth out of the remains of that which comes previously. If I did not, can you imagine the overcrowding that would exist? Nothing would survive, in the end, if everything were to live forever. It's an interesting paradox," he answered gently.

"It seems strange to me that everything we try to make people fear we do with threats of you," the old man mused.

"Well, that is understandable," the gentleman said with a grin. "Humanity has an obsession with form over substance. I myself am an inevitability. On a long enough timeline, I am unavoidable, but there are definitely choices available that push our meeting time further down the line. People very seldom take their mortality seriously until they have come face-to-face with it. When they do it is invariably with dread and incomprehension. As I said, I am an end result. The processes that lead to me are the choices people make in their everyday lives. A lot of times, choice isn't even a part of the equation. There is somewhat of a balance involved in choice and 'accident,' but it all depends on how careless one wants to be with what one has."

"Is there an afterlife?" asked the elderly man apprehensively, as he placed his empty cup on the tray and refilled it. The kind gentleman before him declined a second cup.

"You did call me, so therefore I assume you are ready and willing to find out. Yes, he is waiting for you, somewhere," he answered, reading the old man's mind and looking at the curled-up kitten figurine by the window.

"He was a good man," the elderly gentleman said, looking in the same direction, then glancing up at a black-and-white picture on the mantle. In it he stood with his husband, some forty years ago, at their wedding. They were both in long-tailed tuxedos, beaming at their families, with Champagne glasses raised in a toast. How young they were, he thought, remembering those times fondly.

"He still is. Handsome as ever as well. He did worry so much about you when I came for him. He cared more about you than he did about where he was going. That is really quite rare, you know. He watches over you always, my dear," said the gentleman, in all seriousness, leaning forward.

The elderly man nodded in agreement and relief, then pushed himself upright from his rocking chair. He headed to the windowsill and blew out the candle. He looked at the gentleman who stood by his side. Then he turned off the gas handle for the fire in the foyer, extinguishing it, then turned off the lights in the kitchen. He walked to the front door, handed Mr. Dark his long, flowing jacket, and took a warm parka for himself. He slipped on his winter boots and stepped out into the cold night, where the snowflakes seemed to invite him to dance. Death gave him his hand, and they departed. Inside the cold, dark house, the heart of the pendulum had stopped.

To my great-uncles, both still living, who, because of their many decades together show us all the meaning of being a loving couple.

The Stars, Like Visions

Igor Gorgoff could not have been, by any stretch of the imagination, considered a kind man. He believed in a grim pater familias role in the implementation of tyrannical rule in his own home. He was the master and held no qualms about reminding his mate and offspring of this fact whenever he deigned to open his mouth. His family, therefore, constantly catered to his every twisted whim. They attempted to remain invisible the rest of the time to keep him from commenting in his usually violent-tempered manner. On the rare occasion that he smiled, his face was unrecognizable, as the crevice that opened horizontally shone with a preternatural lugubriousness that made all those who witnessed it shudder and recoil. The tightrope his family had to cross on a daily basis was a draining one, both emotionally and physically.

Matters were aggravated somewhat by the complete randomness of Igor's outbursts. There was no pattern one could discern in the events that set him off. It was as if the simple act of breathing could somehow touch a deep and sensitive nerve that made him lose his mind, throwing off a volley of invectives toward his closest victims. Of his four children, two boys and two girls, half already had fled the hell of home and kept tenuous relations with the rest of the family. The two youngest, Anastasia and Yegor, not yet being of age to follow their elder brother and sister in exile, bided their time until they too could find a safe haven.

It was with utter surprise, then, that their father announced one fine April day that they would be leaving the city for the evening to witness the beauty of a meteor shower. They would head to the low hills a few miles from their home in Grand Forks, North Dakota, he decreed. The confusion was great within the clan, as the announcement regarding the evening's entertainment did not involve their father's usual drunken rants and reprimands. Their typically demure mother seemed unnaturally excited and did not even appear to care about his two angry outbursts. Even though apprehension was high, there was a hope that this night might be relaxing for once, rather than the tear-filled and harrowing evenings that had preceded it. Departure time was 6 o'clock sharp, and everyone was loaded into the family car, father, mother, and two antsy kids.

Yegor was only twelve years old but was wizened beyond his age, having had his childhood stabbed and beaten repeatedly until he had been forced to leave it behind and find shelter within a shell of grim emotionless-ness. He tried to fiercely protect his five-year-old sister, Anastasia, as best he could, to spare her from suffering a similar fate. Even at that young age, she too was beginning to acquire the characteristic disillusionment that marked the Gorgoff children.

Yegor became worried as they drove toward the city limits in the deepening sunset. His initial, if mild, enthusiasm quickly had been squelched. He had a natural distrust of everything his father did, especially what could loosely be termed as kindness. This situation felt thoroughly out of whack with what he knew of his father's personality and demeanor. The fact that they were on their way to a secluded area outside the city did not bode well with him. The outcome of this expedition they were undertaking smelled ranker than anything he'd had to endure in his short and brutish life. He could not dare to venture a guess toward the endnote of this present course. There was absolutely no doubt in his mind, however, that it would end badly, but the degree to which this was so was what he feared to face. Any third-hand observer would have felt the same, he thought. He and the rest of his family had learned very early to keep their emotions in check, simply from a survival point of view. Yegor was having a terrible time of it at the moment, feeling a raging headache, his stomach in knots, and his armpits suppurating with a strong and noxious brew. He looked at his younger sister, who sat next to him in the seat behind their mother. She looked so pale and frail. She was staring intently at her shoes when she suddenly turned toward him and gave him a weak smile.

"It's OK," Anastasia said.

She held out her hand to him, and he took it, mentally giving her all his strength. His stomach calmed a bit, and his headache seemed to dissipate. He then noticed their father staring at them with slitted eyes in the rearview mirror, and he could not suppress a shudder. They left the city limits in the deepening dusk, and the outline of the dark trees along the road contrasted sharply with the orange sky above. Inside the car hung a ghostly silence, punctured only by the occasional bump in the road. Yegor stared out the window at the passing headlights of cars coming from the other direction. The sky was almost completely black now, with a pale blue band hanging above the trees.

After half-an-hour of driving, they turned on to the dirt road that marked the entrance of the national park. The crunching of stones and the jostle of the car on the uneven path punctuated the complete darkness around them. They arrived at a metal gate a few minutes later. The car came to a stop before it, and the elder Gorgoff stepped out, heading to it and opening it wide, his great girth amplified by the headlights. He returned to the car and drove through, not bothering to close the gate. Yegor looked back at the gate as it faded in the distance. He felt as if they had crossed a threshold, a point of no return.

For five minutes they climbed the hillside steadily, following the chaotic road. These were ancient and eroded hills, not mountains. The top was barren of trees, a perfect place to view the sky. There was a picnic table a bit farther from the car; it was a color a few shades lighter than forest green. The car was turned off, as well as the headlights, and the whole family took this as a sign to exit the vehicle.

The cold air was fresh and smelled of pine. Yegor was glad he had thought to wear his tuque and gloves. New weeds were beginning to grow, and the long wild grasses were starting to poke their heads out of the ground. Spring was on its way, and all the snow had melted away. Yegor walked sullenly toward the picnic table, taking his sister by the hand and sitting her next to him when he had found it. Rather than sit on the seat, he did so directly on the table. He made sure to face his father, so that in the event that things went awry, he would see him coming.

Igor Gorgoff paid no attention to his family. His gaze was fixed firmly on the night sky, which was devoid of clouds. The stars, this far away from the city, were brilliant and innumerable. His face lacked expression, as he buried his hands deep inside the pockets of his thick jacket. As Yegor stared toward the bulky outline of his father, his attention was drawn to the sky by a streak of light, then another. Soon the night sky was filled with shooting stars. The sight transfixed him. His fingers traced the carved messages in the wooden picnic table. In the darkness a light snow surprisingly began to fall. As Yegor stared into the night, the heavens illuminated by brilliant flashes, the soft, cool down of winter's last breath enveloped him. For a moment he was elsewhere. He forgot about all of his troubles, all of his pain, all of his sorrow. He forgot about his father.

His father, though, had not forgotten about them. He was walking slowly, as quietly as possible, toward his children, who were staring at the sky. He held a sharp, silver, bloody thing in his right hand.

When he heard a boot crushing the gravel near him, Yegor came back to reality as a sleepwalker might when awoken at the moment of stepping off a cliff. When he saw that his father was coming nearer, he instinctively looked for his mother. He could not see her outline in the darkness and decided to run, taking his sister with him.

"Run, Ana!" he whispered.

The little girl complied, needing no more explanation. As they began their escape, they heard their father running after them and bellowing to stop. He kept yelling louder, but as they got farther away, his yelling and insults became more like screams of terror and agonizing gurgles. They headed straight for the trees and veered left, trying to make their path of escape as confusing as possible for their deranged father. A few seconds later, they stopped, realizing there was no pursuit. They lay under some brush, in the darkness, for several minutes. They stared, shivering, in the direction of the car and their father's last known whereabouts but could hear nothing that would indicate that he was after them. Their hearts raced wildly, and they tried to dissimulate their panting breaths in their mitts.

Anastasia had begun to cry softly, yet still there did not seem to be anyone coming to get them. Yegor told her to stay put and headed up the slope to attempt to see what was happening. He heard two sounds going toward the top of the hill. One was a low gurgle, the other a pained grunting. He found the author of the first and identified it as that of his father. He was lying on his back. Yegor quickly got up and began to look for the source of the second sound, which he knew would be his mother. He found her near the car. She was lying on her side, clutching her stomach. She groaned softly and muttered something under her breath. Yegor reached out to her and called her name. She recoiled at the touch, but when she realized her son was with her, she whimpered and called his name.

"Yegor! I'm so sorry! Where is Ana? *Where is your father?*" she cried, sobbing.

"It's OK now, Mom. We're OK!" he told her. He stroked her face and kissed her cheek. He went to the car, and as he had hoped, the keys were in the ignition. He turned the key to activate the headlights, then stepped out of the car. His mother was curled up in front of it, clutching her bloody stomach. There was blood on her face as well, and Yegor noticed he had some of his mother's blood on his mitts too. He went to her and asked what he could do. She was bleeding from her stomach, so he took off his jacket and wrapped it tightly around her. He got her up and into the backseat of the car with the last bit of energy she had; then she passed out. He walked over to his father, who was now silent, a few meters past the picnic table. His face was covered in black semi-transparent bubbles.

Yegor headed to the edge of the hill and called out to his sister. After a few moments, he saw her head pop up, a bit to his left, from the bushes where they had been hiding. He noticed now that what was raining from the sky was not snow but a dark soot that seemed to melt on contact with the ground. He signaled for Anastasia to come. She climbed the steep hill and had stopped crying now that the moment of crisis had ended. Her cheeks were dirty with the black soot and streaked with tears.

They hurried over to their father, who was splayed, apparently lifeless, on the cold gravel. Yegor knelt to get a better look at his father's face. The dark bubbles seemed to be slowly devouring him, inside and out. Suddenly one of them erupted, and a cloud of dark smoke was ejected from it. They both recoiled from the grisly sight. After swift yet careful consideration, Yegor realized there was no way they could take their father with them. He was simply too large for him to drag to the car. Besides, whatever was afflicting him might spread.

Yegor took his sister by the hand, and they returned to the car. He knew he didn't have much time to help his mother. He sat his sister in the front passenger's seat and went to his mother to try to wake her up. She came to briefly, and Yegor wrapped seatbelts over his mother so she would not move too much during transportation. He turned the ignition key and started the engine. In the headlights he could see his father's body losing cohesion. The black bubbles that had covered his face now seemed to come from under his clothing as well, eating him from the inside. Yegor had thought he might feel bitter satisfaction over his father's demise, if it ever happened, but all he felt now was a kind of pity and sadness.

His sister looked at him and whispered, "He tried to kill us."

Yegor nodded with grim intensity and put the car in reverse. This was a terrible time to learn how to drive, but he had no choice. His mother's life depended on it. As he began to follow the only path that led down the hillside, he thought about whatever had killed his father. He wondered what it could have been and where it had come from. He thought he might never be able to erase the memory of his father's eaten face. As the car bounced along the road, their mother groaned and would regain consciousness briefly in the backseat. Yegor had turned on the heat as high as possible, since his mother was wearing his jacket around her waist but didn't have on a coat of her own. His sister told their mother in a soft voice that everything would be fine. Her answers were generally whimpers and apologies.

Once Yegor had found the main road, he accelerated to a breakneck speed, heading toward the city and the nearest hospital. Fortunately he remembered the way there from the multiple times he'd had to go there because of his father's pummeling.

As they arrived in the parking lot, they saw there was a throng of people waiting to be admitted outside the hospital. Cars had been abandoned everywhere inside the overflowing parking lot. Not being able to wait, he stopped the car as close as he could to the hospital and got his mother to stand up. With her leaning on him, they walked the hundred or so yards to the emergency entrance. They pushed their way past the others, who gave way at the sight of so much blood. Inside it was chaos; paramedics, doctors, and nurses were racing in every direction. Yegor went to the first person who was standing still and got her attention. The wild-eyed nurse looked at him, then at his mother, saw the blood coming from under his coat, and called for a stretcher. Two paramedics showed up thirty seconds later. They lay her down on the stretcher with professional care then wheeled her away. He followed with his sister as best he could, but when they went into the operating room, he was told they had to wait outside.

He sat his sister on the chair next to his and retrieved a coloring book from the stack of magazines. Most of the illustrations were already scribbled on by the hundreds of children who must have gotten their hands on it before them, but he finally found one page that was mostly still virginal. With the only crayon he could find (orange), she began to meticulously and patiently fill in the clown picture.

Yegor looked around the hallway and took note of the insane speed at which most patients were being wheeled about by the overworked staff. It was not the usual activity, obviously. He noticed the floor was covered in a fine coat of black dust. He looked at himself and saw that he too was covered in dust, as was his sister. A bulky television on the wall was turned to a news channel, and the male announcer was somewhere outside, where hundreds of people were running every which way. Occasionally one would fall to the ground, never to rise again. Yegor glanced around and saw that someone had left the remote control for the television lying on a chair. He turned up the volume, and the reporter was beginning to grow frantic, as in the background more and more people were falling to the ground, writhing in pain.

"As you can see, the scene is devastating, and we have taken refuge atop this building to avoid being trampled. No one knows for certain the cause of what is happening, but as of one hour ago, a fine powder began to fall from the sky, immediately preceded by the projected meteor shower," he explained, seemingly trying to maintain his professional demeanor. "All these people you see behind me were at the Minnetonka rock concert we were covering earlier when this tragedy happened. There is no word yet from authorities, but we strongly recommend that our viewers stay home and keep calm."

The camera panned to one of the fallen victims, and Yegor heard the announcer say to the cameraperson, "Are you getting this?" The person they were zooming in on was wriggling on the ground as black bubbles burst out of her mouth, covering her face. Panic obviously finally overtook the news anchor, because Yegor heard him exclaim, "Oh, my God!" over and over, until he too was making those horrible gurgling sounds Yegor's father had made before succumbing. The last thing he saw on television was the camera being dropped by the cameraperson, being knocked sideways, and taking a last shot of the anchor's face, eyes wide with fear, bubbles pouring out of his mouth. Yegor looked intensely at the television, then at Anastasia, who was no longer coloring but returning his gaze.

"They shouldn't panic, you know. It only makes it worst." She was right, of course.

He turned off the TV and began to look for someone in authority, to warn them. He realized, though, that no one would listen to him, so he sat back down. All around him, people were dying from fear, and there was nothing he could do about it. So he accepted the situation and waited.

A few hours later, when they both remembered they were famished, he took his sister to the cafeteria, bringing with him his mother's purse. He was sure she wouldn't mind. As they entered, he saw that the room was completely empty. There wasn't even a person working behind the counter. He asked his sister what she wanted and found her a suitable cold sandwich from the refrigerator. He took egg salad, and she had pastrami. They both took orange juice and an apple. Yegor went behind the counter and counted approximately how much money he needed to pay for all the food and left it next to the cash register. They went and sat in a corner by the window. Many of the chairs were overturned, as if whoever did not absolutely need to be at the hospital had run away, which they had. They could barely hear the insane rush that was happening in the rest of the hospital, and were glad for it. When they were done eating, Yegor took his sister to the washroom and cleaned her up, scrubbing her as best he could to remove the soot that covered her from head to toe; then he tried to do the same with himself. He then found a couch in a corner of the cafeteria, and they both fell asleep almost instantly from exhaustion.

When they awoke the next day, it was because a security guard had found them while doing his rounds. Yegor hurriedly brought his sister back to the last place they had seen their mother before she had been brought through the doors to the operating room. He asked a doctor who was walking by what had happened to her, and after several minutes of discussion with a pastel-green-clad nurse at a desk, he returned to the children with the devastating news.

"I'm sorry, children, but your mother passed away. Is there anyone we can call for you?" he asked, empathizing.

"My...my brother and sister," Yegor answered, his voice cracking.

The doctor handed him a pen and paper, and through tear-filled eyes, Yegor wrote down his older brother and sister's names and phone numbers. He sat back down on the chair where he had spent part of the previous evening and wept quietly with his sister. When the tears had subsided somewhat, he turned on the television. The announcer said that the phenomenon that had occurred the previous night had been worldwide. As panic had increased, so had the death toll. In all, 90 percent of those infected were reported to be dead or dying, their bodies eaten by whatever was inside them. As well, matters were complicated by the fact that every bubble, when burst, unleashed new toxin that was carried by the wind to other unsuspecting victims. The dead were everywhere but were swiftly evaporating, as if they had never existed.

The hospital was fairly quiet this morning. Everyone seemed very calm but conscious that the flash plague they had witnessed might not be over. As in the case of an earthquake, they expected aftershocks that might take them even though the main temblor had not. The doctor took them to see their mother one last time. She had been one of the few who had not passed away because of the black soot. Yegor and Anastasia looked at their mother intently, kissed her on her cold cheek, and said goodbye. Yegor held Ana in his arms and walked out of the room, as they both wept.

Their older brother came to pick them up two hours later. He told them their older sister had not lived through the night either. He went to see his mother and paid his last respects as well. Driving away from the hospital, they could see the utter carnage the outbreak had caused. The roads were covered with damaged, empty cars, the windows plastered within with the remains of their owners, gone back to dust. Minimal and improvised fire crews worked as hard as they could to put out blazes that had been set in the panic. A jumbo jet had crash-landed in the neighborhood shortly after takeoff. Its trail of destruction could be followed in a straight line, like a furrow that had been plowed through a block of homes, ending in a blazing wreck. Through all of this insanity, the three in the car remained calm.

For a week the siblings did not speak much, except to relate what had happened to each of them on that fateful night. Their older brother apologized for not having been able to remove them from their family home sooner. He was forgiven. They spent their days trying to help out with the clean-up of the now mostly empty city, and that is what they were doing on the day that the enormous oblong ships began to descend, calmly, silently, from the clouds.

Adeena's Pet

Adeena lived alone with her blind uncle on the outskirts of Kabul. Still too young to be married, she spent her days helping her uncle hawk his copper kettles at the diminutive shop he owned on Victory Avenue. The street had been renamed after the Russian expulsion, but the irony of so many foreign invaders patrolling was lost on no one. Adeena had come to live with her uncle after a suicide bomber had killed her parents near their mosque two years ago. The mosque had been close to a strategic target, namely a NATO building. The guards had been able to kill the driver of the explosive-laden car as it sped toward them, but this had resulted in the car swerving into the building next to it, an outdoor market filled with shoppers. Adeena's parents were coming out of Friday prayers when they were hit with shrapnel. They were not the only victims that day, but they were the ones who mattered most to Adeena, who was only six at the time. Her brother, Kaihan, had run away to join the Taliban the year before, so she had been taken in by her uncle, who had lost his sight when he had been walking with friends too near a landmine, it would seem.

Business was never brisk. The economy was terrible, and there was always the chance someone would take advantage of a large crowd to detonate himself or herself. Indeed there had not been any direct attack on the capital in the past few weeks, but this was no indication of the ceasing of hostilities. Adeena and Uncle Kosha had enough to survive, but little more resources to their names. They inhabited the small back area of the shop, which comprised two rooms. The bedroom was Adeena's, and she loved her uncle dearly for having given up his comfortable mattress by the window for her. He slept by the fireplace in the other room, usually on the floor. After every day of work in the front shop selling kettles, and having eaten a bit of food, Uncle Kosha would settle next to the stove and hammer pieces of copper into kettles. Adeena would fall asleep to the sharp sound of a ball-peen hammer striking the copper on an anvil. It had become her lullaby, and she wondered how she could ever fall asleep without it. Sometimes, when she was unable to sleep, she snuck out the window of her room. She would climb over the wall of their backyard to sit with her back against it and stare out at the desert night. This was a dangerous thing to do, though, and she never stayed out very long.

Every morning she'd wake up to find her uncle asleep on the floor, next to one or two new kettles. She would fetch coal from behind the house, in the tiny locked shed, and start a fire in the little stove. She would then take a metal bucket to the public fountain and pump some water. Then she would return home and fill their kettle with water, boil it, and make tea. By this time her uncle would have woken and would prepare breakfast for both of them. They would then go out back and use some of the hot water to wash their faces. Breakfast was always a simple affair—a bit of bread, perhaps some nuts and raisins or dates. They would then sit under the faded red tent in front of the shop and wait for customers, sipping strong black tea while the blazing Afghani sun hazed and shimmered. This was Adeena's life, and what she expected to live for a very long time.

One night, after a particularly long and boring day, Adeena was unable to sleep. She did not like long and boring days, since she had too much time to think. This always got her to thinking about her parents and brother, which brought her to her present predicament. She listened for a very long time to the keening sound of the hammer on copper, as she tossed and turned under her blanket. Sleep would not come. She silently slipped out from under the blanket and peered through the crack of the tent that separated her room from where her uncle was making a pot. She smiled sadly, picking up her blanket and sandals, and went out the window of her room. The moon was almost full, and she shivered in the cold air. She found the old wooden crate she used to go over the wall and deftly climbed up it. She looked around in every direction but saw no one skulking around. She dangled her blanket to the ground to see whether anything dangerous would scurry or slither away. Satisfied that no creatures were directly below her, she hopped over the wall. She landed without a sound and inspected the area around the wall to make sure it was devoid of any unfriendly fauna that might have had taken up domicile there for the night. There were no scorpions or snakes that she could see. The ground and wall were cold, so she slipped on her sandals and wrapped herself in her warm blanket.

The surrounding hills of Kabul were hardscrabble rock interspersed with sand. It was nowhere near as beautiful as the Sahara, which Adeena had seen in a documentary video a very long time ago, it seemed. In the far distance were the mountains, and somewhere among them, her brother was playing a deadly game of hide-and-seek with the foreign invaders. Maybe he was already dead. She had no way of knowing. She sighed and looked up at the moon again. It was immense in the sky above her. She felt that if she jumped she might be able to touch it.

She was suddenly startled by a sound that came from a garbage heap not three feet away. She was getting ready to climb up the wall, for fear she would get attacked by some wild animal, when she heard a sad mewling from the same direction where the movement had originated. She paused and heard a short sobbing sound, like that of a wounded animal. Her curiosity was piqued, and she slowly crept toward the sound in a circumspect way, so as to surprise whatever it was from behind. She heard the mewling again, and she stopped, dead in her tracks, her heart beating so fast she felt it thump in her ears. She waited for what felt an eternity but then found her courage again. Slowly she crept forward, craning her neck to the side, to try to spy what had made those bizarre noises. Suddenly a head popped up from inside a garbage bag.

Adeena was so shocked that she fell backward on her behind. The tiny creature was no larger than a scorpion and had large black eyes. It had brownish skin; its neck was a stalk; and it looked sideways at Adeena, seemingly sizing her up. She began to back away from it on her bum, but as she made a gesture, the creature went back into hiding. She stopped, and the wide-eyed thing peered up from the garbage again, very slowly. It made the same mewling sound it had before, and Adeena saw that within its pink mouth were two rows of very pointy little teeth. She was scared motionless.

The little creature dashed out of the bag at incredible speed, and before she could turn and run, it was rubbing its head against her sandal. She looked at it without moving for a moment. Its body was light-brown, and it had six legs. On each leg was what looked like tiny little hands, each with stubby fingers. Its head was separated from its body by a long, thin neck, and it had a long tail, very much like a lizard's, that swayed back and forth. It was sniffing her foot now and gave a cute little sneeze, which made Adeena giggle. The small being seemed to possess powers of mimicry and made a sound that was a lot like her giggle. Adeena felt herself relax, and the being rubbed its head lovingly against her foot once more. She slowly, and very gently, placed her hand near the being, and it smelled it, its tiny nostrils flaring. It began to lick her hand, and she reached down to the ground to pick it up. The little creature readily climbed into her hand. She realized that it was getting late and that she was feeling chilled, so she placed the being she had found on her shoulder, where it cozied up to her neck. She found the discarded crutch she always used to climb back over the wall, placed it in the usual spot, climbed over, and knocked the crutch down. She then climbed down the wall and snuck into her room. She slipped into her bed and felt a bit of joy at having found a new friend. Then she fell into a deep sleep, filled with dreams of her parents.

The next morning Adeena woke up feeling refreshed and alive. She hopped out of bed with a song on her lips, which she hummed very low, so as not to wake her uncle. She did not know the words, but it was a beautiful and melodic rhapsody that reminded her of the stars and faraway places. She then remembered what had happened the night before and wondered if she had dreamt it. She looked around her bed, but her friend wasn't there. She went out back to fetch more coal, and when she opened the stove to put it inside, she was startled by a movement underneath. She quickly realized that her new pet had slipped under the stove for warmth. It made sense, she thought; if it was a lizard, it needed more heat than other creatures. She filled up the stove but accidently dropped a large piece of coal. The little brown creature pounced on it and took it back under the stove.

Adeena was curious to know what it could possibly want with a piece of smelly coal, so she peered under the stove. She was amazed to see the little being wrap its small mouth around the giant chunk! She was afraid it would harm itself, but as she reached under the stove to try to retrieve the piece, the creature emitted what was unmistakably a threatening sound. Adeena instantly pulled her hand back. She hoped her friend knew what it was doing. She didn't want it to poison itself. She lit the stove and continued to do her daily duties. She decided it would not be prudent to speak to her uncle about her find, for fear he would tell her to give it away or take it back to the desert or worse. She knew they had very limited means, but she didn't want to lose her new pet. She had very much fallen in love with this adorable little being.

She went about her day as if nothing had changed. It was very difficult for her to stay calm, thinking that she had a playmate waiting for her in the other room. She kept looking at the clock and waiting for the sun to set. When finally it did, she had to force herself to slow down while eating her supper. She kissed her uncle goodnight and went straight to bed. The usually comforting hammering coming from the other room seemed unbearably long to her that night. Eventually it ceased, and she waited a bit longer to be certain her uncle truly was sleeping. She peered through the tent and saw he was curled up near the stove, his newest creations resting near him. She oh so carefully crept to the stove, which gave off a very somber orange light. By the light of the dying embers, she knelt by the side of the stove and squinted her eyes to see her little friend. She saw a faint red light in the shape of a small ball coming from below. In the dim light, she thought she saw the creature move. She tried to reach for it, but once again she heard a low growl. Afraid that her uncle would wake if she insisted too much, she crept back to her bed, saddened that she had not been able to play, even a little bit, with her friend. She lay down and covered herself with her blanket, telling herself that it was all right; she would have the chance some other day. As she fell asleep, she felt a drop slide down her cheek on to her pillow.

Adeena's dreams were confusing that night. Her parents were not her parents, but they were. They had missed her very much, but they seemed to tower over her. She somehow felt as if she could be with them. It made no sense, and she woke up feeling a bit tired and groggy. She got up and performed her usual duties, but in a daze, as if on automatic pilot. The day's heat seemed more suffocating than before. That night she felt a bit on edge as she crept to the stove. When she peered underneath, the thing came flying out of darkness and licked her face. She noticed, though, that there was something under the stove that had not been there before. It gave off a kind of glint, and she reached under, very carefully, so as not to touch the bottom of the burning stove. She slowly removed her arm from beneath, and when she brought her dirty hand to her face and opened it, she could not believe her eyes. She could not for an instant believe that what she held in her hand was truly what she thought it was.

She gulped, very slowly, so as not to make a sound, and walked on the tips of her toes back to her room. She carried her pet on her shoulder, where he eyed her hand with apprehension. She slid under her blanket, and poking her head out again, she held her hand up to her face. She very gently opened her fingers. In the palm of her hand was an unthinkable object. She held a very finely cut diamond, and a fairly large one at that. Her eyes were as wide as saucers. She realized her pet was magical.

"I will call you Djinn," Adeena whispered to it, in honor of the ancient genies that populated the forbidden legends.

"Dzeeeen," he whispered back.

She lay her head down on her pillow and fell asleep. During the night, she thought she heard dogs barking in the distance. She dreamt of faraway places that night and slept very well indeed.

The next morning, Djinn was nowhere to be found, and she guessed he had returned to his hiding place under the stove. She went to the back and gathered coal but thought she would not have to do it for very much longer. She went to get a bucket of water and imagined a house with running water. As she and her uncle washed themselves, though, he asked her, "Did you notice, Adee, that we have a visitor in the house?"

She feigned surprise and said no, she had not noticed.

"Some sort of wild creature has elected domicile under the stove. I shall have to kill it," he said, looking grave.

"No! Don't kill him!" she yelled, and immediately regretted it.

Her uncle smiled. "What is this creature, Adee? What did you bring home the other night?"

He knew. There was no way she could hide it from him. She told him the story of how she had adopted her new pet, as well as the incredible discovery she had made, and the blind uncle listened attentively to every word. Finally she asked, "How did you know, Uncle Kosha?"

"I'm blind, child, not deaf. You can keep your little Djinn, but you must be very careful. There are some very dangerous people about, and they would love to use this unusual being for their own nefarious purposes. We must keep him well hidden. As for the diamond, I don't know how we will be able to sell it. Let me think about it."

He ruffled her hair. She smiled and gave him a big kiss on the cheek. They let their day carry on as it normally would, but as the night came, they went to the stove, and Adeena called out to Djinn. He came out, slowly, and looked at Uncle Kosha as he neared the edge of the stove.

"It's OK, Djinn. Come out!" Adeena said.

"Dzeen!" he responded then went to her uncle and rubbed his head against the old man's ankles.

Adeena bent down and looked under the stove. She put her hand underneath, and when she took it back out again, she did not have one big diamond but many little ones. She placed the diamonds into her uncle's hands, and he sifted them from one to the other.

"There is a small fortune here," he mused. "We must go to the warlord and see if he wants to buy them. No one else could afford diamonds, and trying to sell them around town would definitely attract the wrong kind of attention. We will go tomorrow."

That night he did not hammer any new copper pots or kettles, and the silence in the house was eerie. Adeena had a hard time falling asleep, but Djinn was curled up next to her ear, and he emanated a soothing essence that helped her relax and fall into beautiful dreams.

The next morning they put some coal into the stove for Djinn and lit the fire. They gathered the diamonds in an old plastic bag, and Uncle Kosha put them in his pocket. They left early so they could be back before the midday heat pummeled down on Kabul. They walked for three hours on mostly deserted roads that were lined on each side with poppy plants and marijuana, the source of the Afghani warlord's wealth. As they approached the large compound of Esfandyar Abd el Nasrallah, armed guards came to meet them. They were solidly built soldiers, muscular and alert, not at all the kind of men you would mess around with. Adeena led her blind uncle by the arm, and he held his walking stick with the other. The guards questioned them, and they said they had some very important business with Master Nasrallah. The guards searched them for weapons and explosives, and when they were satisfied that the pair were harmless, they led them into the interior of the compound.

On every rampart stood an armed guard. In every nook, every cranny, seemed to stand an emotionless, motionless statue resembling a man and carrying a Russian automatic weapon. The interior of the compound stood in stark contrast to the desert without. It was like an ancient and decadent castle, with an interior oasis and fountain. The first floor was all arches, with intricately decorated frescoes and classical Arabic written everywhere in gold. Palm trees lined a shallow yet expansive pool, and the tiles at its bottom were an opalescent indigo. The guards escorted Adeena and her uncle to the main house, where they were met by a grey-tweed-suit-clad gentleman in his forties who announced himself to be Mr. Nasrallah's secretary and lawyer, Mr. Fahran Essad.

"*Salaam aleikum*, Essad *effendi*. My name is Kosha," said Uncle Kosha.

"*Aleikum salaam*," answered the man. "What is it exactly we can do for you today, Mr. Kosha?" He looked over them both with a toothy grin.

"We have come to speak to your master, Essad *effendi*. Would it be possible to gain audience with the esteemed Esfandyar Abd el Nasrallah?" Uncle Kosha asked deferentially.

"I am sorry, but the great Esfandyar Nasrallah is quite occupied at the moment, you understand. He sent me to take care of less pressing business," he said, looking very inconvenienced.

"I am sorry to hear that, Essad *effendi*. I had hoped to increase the wealth and prestige of your master, Nasrallah, but it seems this will not be possible. Good day, sir," Uncle Kosha said, looking dejected, and signaled for Adeena to turn them around and get going, as the interview seemed to be at an end.

"Wait. Just a moment," the secretary said, and he took a cell phone from his back pocket. He spoke briefly into the receiver and looked somewhat pained when he hung up.

"My master will see you now," he said between gritted teeth.

"Thank you for your kindness, sir," Uncle Kosha said, bowing.

Adeena could not help smiling at her uncle's ruse. Great wooden doors opened before them, and they were taken inside the fortress's mansion. A wall of fresh air greeted them as they entered. Exotic birds of all colors and shapes chirped, warbled, and trilled in large cages along the corridor. A blood-red carpet softened the sound of their footsteps, and they walked briskly to a spiral staircase, along whose wall hung what must have been the entire Nasrallah lineage in oil paintings — all save the last image, which was a large photograph of the most recent inheritor of the land. He stood with his right foot on a tiger's head, which was visibly stuffed, and held in his right hand the same kind of Russian-made automatic weapon as his guards possessed. He was bearded, chin held high, lips tight, and did not seem to harbor a single ounce of humor. Adeena's eyes were locked on the portrait of the man, but Uncle Kosha, unable to see it, kept walking up the stairs.

At the top of the stairs, Essad led them to the right, then a short distance down another wide corridor with shaded windows, and finally to an immense room lined with intricately sewn cushions against every wall. Tall, thin windows let in diffuse and multicolored light through gorgeous stained glass. Two guards stood at attention on either side of the doors, but they gave no notice to the two insignificant pleaders who had come to bother their master. A large man with a jet-black beard and camouflage clothing sat at the far end of the room. A terribly loud silence hung in the air, and Adeena felt her hands shake as she walked toward the scowling man across the way. Uncle Kosha put his hand on her shoulder, and she looked up to him, relaxing a bit. She saw that two cushions had been placed on the carpeted floor, five feet from the man, and these they approached.

"My liege!" announced Essad loudly, startling Adeena. "These people asked for a private audience."

Esfandyar Abd el Nasrallah nodded gravely and looked at both of his visitors with a penetrating gaze. "The laws of Islam and charity command it," he said. "Speak, and tell me what you would like of me, Mister..." He let the word hang in the air.

"Kosha, sir. I am sorry, but you have been misinformed. It is not what you may do for us, but what we may do for you," said Uncle Kosha, with eyes downcast.

"Truly? And what do you believe you can do for me, Mr. Kosha?" Esfandyar Nasrallah said, beginning to be curious.

It was at that moment that a young man entered carrying a tray with black tea. Adeena almost got up to her feet when she recognized her brother, Kaihan. He looked at her in the eye and very carefully shook his head "No!" and she restrained herself as best she could. Meanwhile, Uncle Kosha had retrieved the small bag of diamonds from his hidden pocket and was handing them to Mr. Nasrallah's secretary. No one else had seen Adeena and her brother's exchange of glances. With a quizzical look, Mr. Essad took the old plastic bag and handed it to his master, who accepted the dirty bag with a disgusted air. He then opened it, wanting to put an end to this charade, but inside saw the shiny glint of the promise of even greater wealth. He paused.

"Where did you find these?" he finally asked, curious as to how such a poor man could have gotten his hands on such a treasure.

"I am sorry, Effendi, but I cannot reveal my sources," answered Uncle Kosha, taking a sip of tea.

"You are a cheeky fellow, sir. Fine. I will give you a fair price for these. Fahran, take care of these two, will you?" and on these words, the discussion was over.

Uncle Kosha got up, as did Adeena. When she looked around, her brother was nowhere to be seen. The secretary led them out of the room, and they were taken back down the same stairs. When they walked back to the entrance, though, four guards appeared and took Adeena and Kosha under each arm.

"What is the meaning of this?" barked Uncle Kosha.

"You are being taken care of," Essad said with a smile.

He led them to a large wooden door, which he unlocked.

Stone stairs led down into the darkness, and Essad ordered the guards to take them to a cell. The stairwell smelled of must and age, as well as a few other less pleasant things. Adeena was crying, wondering what would happen to them. They were both placed into a cell, cold and damp, where far above Adeena spotted a single tiny window. The window was too high and too small to climb through, and Adeena curled up on a straw mattress in the corner and wept silently.

"It will be all right, Adeena. Don't worry," Uncle Kosha promised, his voice unsteady. "They won't hurt us too much until they find out where we got those diamonds."

"I saw Kaihan!" she exclaimed, wiping a tear from her eye.

"You saw your brother? Where?" asked Uncle Kosha, incredulous.

"He served our tea!"

He smiled in the darkness. "Maybe not all is lost then."

A few hours later, as they pondered plans of escape and means of eluding their captors, they heard a soft mewling from above.

"Djinn!" cried Adeena.

"Dzeeeen!" answered her friend, from above, against the window that led outside.

"Uncle, Djinn followed us!" she said with a laugh.

Djinn imitated her giggle, and he scrambled down the wall, as quick as could be. Soon Adeena was holding her darling in her hands, and he was cooing like a baby.

"What do we do now, Djinn?" she asked, peering into his small brown face.

In lieu of an answer, he sniffed the air then jumped out of her hand and under the door of their cell. He soon returned with a lump of coal, which he rolled under the small stove in the corner. Several hours later, Essad returned with several guards, and they took Uncle Kosha away. Adeena was left alone, but she was given a few matches and a few pieces of coal to put in her stove. She did so, and very soon a small fire was blazing inside the potbelly stove. The cells underneath the castle were chilly, and the warmth was more than welcome. Adeena peered underneath the stove, and Djinn was a bright red color and as round as a golf ball. Uncle Kosha was returned to her two hours later. Adeena ran to him and gave him a big hug. He was sweating heavily and seemed to have trouble sitting down.

"It's all right," he said. "They went easy on me this time."

Adeena helped her poor uncle lay on the mattress. They received scraps of food several hours later, and both tried to eat as much as they could. They then curled up on the mattress and attempted to sleep.

When they awoke in the morning, Djinn was curled up on his back, in the middle of the dirty floor, with a shiny, multifaceted new diamond in his upturned paws. The apex of the diamond was pointed straight at the ceiling. His mouth was wide open, and not a sound came from it. Somewhere outside, dogs were barking madly. Adeena tried to get closer, but without moving his body, Djinn looked directly at her and gave her a surly look. She backed away from him without trying to interrupt him further. He kept this position until suddenly he let go of the diamond, turned back onto his paws, and rolled the diamond under the stove. Five seconds later, Essad was opening the door to their cell, and three brutish guards took Uncle Kosha again. Adeena received a bit of cheese for breakfast, and she kept a large share for her uncle. This time they returned much later with him, and when they did, they threw him on the mattress. Adeena ran to her uncle and embraced him, crying warm tears on to his face.

He painfully opened his eyes and smiled at her. "Be strong," he whispered, and he closed his eyes.

He did not open them for the rest of the day, but neither did their captors come to see them again. Djinn rolled his diamond from under the stove once more and lay on his back with it in the exact position as before. Night had fallen, and the moon provided the only light that entered the cell. Djinn opened his mouth, and very soon dogs were barking madly from somewhere outside.

Uncle Kosha woke for a moment and whispered, "Do you hear that, Adee? The melody?"

"No, Uncle. I'm sorry. I can't hear—" But as she said this, a great rumble came from above, and the entire castle began to shake. The dogs were barking like beasts gone mad, and the guards were firing their guns, yelling as they did. A green light flashed repeatedly across their little window, and soon it was shining directly above them from outside.

The door to their cell opened, and Kaihan was standing in the doorway. "We have to leave!" he cried. "The heavens are upon us!"

Adeena ran to her big brother, and he picked her up in his arms, giving her an overwhelming embrace. He then put the little girl down.

"I should never have left home," he said. He went to his uncle and helped him up from the mattress. The man could barely walk, so Kaihan helped him onto his strong back and carried him. Suddenly Kaihan saw Djinn on the floor and exclaimed, "By all that is holy, what is that?"

"That's my Djinn!" retorted Adeena.

Just then the diamond Djinn had been holding burst, and he was showered in smaller ones. He got back to his feet and clambered up Adeena's leg and onto her shoulder. Kaihan made a move to pick up the diamonds, but Adeena told him not to. He hesitated for a moment but then turned to the door, and the three left the cell, along with Djinn. They scrambled up the steps, and as they neared the top, they saw that the entire citadel had been plunged into a supernatural silence. A pale green light shone in the desert night from several points directly above them. The guards were frozen in place, as if time had stopped for them. Their guns were pointed upward, and Adeena was reminded of those ridiculous plastic toy soldiers in various "action" poses she sometimes saw at the market.

Adeena, Kaihan, and Uncle Kosha began to run toward the exit, but three beings suddenly appeared before them, and they paused in midflight. The beings were humanoid but very tall and thin. They wore a kind of reflective clothing and had what looked like very large glass bowls on their heads. It was impossible to see inside the bowls, as they seemed to bubble continuously. Two of the beings were taller than Kaihan and Uncle Kosha, but the third was only slightly taller than Adeena.

Djinn leapt on Adeena's shoulder, squealing, "Zao! Zao! Zaoooooo!"

One of the taller creatures lifted a hand toward Adeena, and she felt as if words and concepts were being inserted into her head but coming from Djinn. She felt what was definitely thankfulness and a warm feeling of love directed toward Djinn. Several concepts she was not able to comprehend appeared in her mind. Since she had no reference words to associate with them, they had a kind of superposition with what she knew that she could try to parse. What she was able to extract from the thought forms was that Djinn was their (daughter's? son's? child's? offspring's?) (pet? companion? friend?) and had escaped during their last scientific mission in the desert. They were (overjoyed? thankful? grateful?) that Adeena had taken such good care of him. They recommended that the group hide, since they had erased the memories of all the armed personnel in the area, and the resulting (chaos? massacre? potential appeasement?) probably would not be to their advantage.

Adeena gave a kiss to Djinn, and the little creature turned a lighter shade of brown for a moment. It rubbed its head against Adeena's cheek then ran down the length of her body toward the smaller being that stood before them. As it drew near its original master, it turned a flaming orange, and the being bent down to pick Djinn up. Djinn ran around the being's body at mad speeds, squealing happily. The trio of visitors, as well as Djinn, then disappeared.

Adeena rapidly explained the coming chaos, and they headed for the front door of the compound. The guards were still frozen, and they were able to slip by without being noticed. When they were a hundred yards from the doors, they turned around to see a shape floating above the citadel. It was larger by far than the castle and hung lazily, pouring green light into the courtyard. Suddenly the lights ceased, and the floating object shot straight into the atmosphere.

A shout was heard. Then another. Then a shot was heard. Very soon the entire compound filled with the sound of gunfire as the guards awoke, not knowing what they were doing there, only that they were armed and surrounded by potentially lethal enemies. They lost no time with idle chitchat and eliminated one another as fast as they could.

Adeena, Kaihan, and Uncle Kosha were accosted one hour later by a Canadian army patrol that had been attracted by the commotion of gunfire and the eerie green lights that had been seen from miles away. They were taken to a NATO base in the area, where Uncle Kosha was treated for the injuries he had sustained at the hands of Esfyandar Abd el Nasrallah and his henchmen.

Kaihan explained that he had been with the Taliban but had run away from them as well. He had seen them do horrible things to people who disagreed with them and no longer considered them the liberators of Afghanistan. They were small-minded thugs, he said, and did not deserve the respect they received. After he had escaped and tried to come home, the roving henchmen of the warlord Nasrallah had captured him. He had been the man's indentured slave for the past two years, with no ability to communicate with the outside. He had heard about the attack that had killed his parents but had not been able to send word to Adeena. From now on he would do all he could to help the broken remnants of his family.

They returned to Kabul a few days later, after they were carefully interrogated about that night's events, then released unharmed. Kaihan remained with his sister and uncle, learning his uncle's trade.

One day, a man was seen wandering down Victory Avenue. He had been wandering the desert for weeks and very much resembled a bag of bones, but it was unmistakably the ex-war-lord. He recognized neither Adeena, Uncle Kosha, or Kaihan, as he walked by them, listlessly. He remembered nothing, either about them or himself.

As she grew older, Adeena realized that she could apply to leave her country, if she wished. She dismissed this option, though, preferring to stay in Kabul. She worked very hard and was allowed to enter the university after she spent years catching up on her lost education. She never forgot her little friend and became one of Afghanistan's most respected female researchers, specializing in crystalline field harmonics. To this day she inspires other young women to excel and sometimes can be spied walking down Victory Road, humming a strange and otherworldly tune, looking to the heavens. As Uncle Kosha liked to say, Djinn had given her something much better than wealth: he had given her knowledge. She would twinkle for the rest of her life with her diamonds of the mind.

The Healing Bride

He looked at her with sadness. The room was dark, save for the light that shone above her bed. She was a pitiful creature, lying there, unconscious. The steady beep of the heart monitor indicated that she was in stable condition. A pump kept air flowing into her cracked ribcage and whispered with every push. It was late, and the hospital staff was nowhere to be seen outside of the room. The lights in the corridors were turned down low. An announcement was heard on the hospital PA system, and then silence, save the mechanical and electronic assistance in the room. Her lips were swollen and cracked, bloody. Her jaw was slightly ajar, in an unnatural position. One of her eyes was black, swollen, and shut. The other was a mess of purplish bruises. Tubes containing feeding solutions had been inserted into her nostrils and arms. A bandage covered her forehead but would soon need to be changed, as blood was beginning to seep through. *This should never have happened*, he thought. It had gone too far.

He was the happiest of men five years earlier, when he had married Sandrine. She was petite, with brown hair and an elfin attitude. He had been certain that she was the woman he would be with for the rest of his life. Unfortunately it seemed this was not to be so. There had been signals that there would be trouble in paradise, but he had ignored them. They came back to the fore several months after the supposed happiest day of his life. She was strong headed and unruly, rarely listening when he spoke to her. It was for her own good that he'd had to put her back in her place. Every single time he had, she had bounced back quite quickly and had seemed to learn her lesson. There were a few occasions when he'd had to "rough her up" after coming back from a night with the boys, because he'd had to endure her pestering. That, she had truly deserved, since what he did with his time was his prerogative. She had no right to question him or even, God forbid, denigrate him for coming home at the hour he desired. Even now he remembered those times with anger and resentment.

There were the times he had wanted to be intimate, but she wouldn't allow him. It seemed as if she never wanted to make love anymore, the bitch. It was with satisfaction that he remembered the times when he had reminded her who wore the pants in their relationship. Of course she had yelled and screamed, but she was his wife—how dare she deny him? There were many times he'd had to set her back on the right path. Every time she had been fine within a day, if a bit more careful and quiet, a lesson learned and internalized.

How she had aged, though, in those five years. Even under the bruises, he saw the lines at the edges of her mouth and eyes. Her hair was cracked and brittle. Since she had cut it short, he could no longer hold her properly from her ponytail when he argued with her. She wasn't as pretty as she used to be. She was so very pale. He sighed and shook his head as he rubbed his temple with his right hand.

What a mess, he thought, over and over again. It was her fault, really. She shouldn't have pissed him off at the top of the stairs. He wouldn't have pushed her down them. So far he was safe, she having gone into a coma as he rushed to the phone to call the ambulance. He had acted appropriately, as the concerned husband, when the police had questioned him about the incident; he even had been able to shed a tear or two (thinking of what might happen if the truth got out). This was now his greatest fear. What would happen when and if she came out of her unconscious state? She would tell the cops, and he might go to jail. There was no way he would let that happen. No chick, not even his wife, would make him go to prison.

He looked around the room and saw that the other hospital bed was free. He went to the door and closed it quietly. Then he slowly turned the rod for the blinds that faced the hallway. He found a pair of latex gloves in a box by the washroom. He went to the other bed and picked up the pillow, fluffing it a bit. He walked over to his wife and looked her over one last time.

They could have been so happy, he thought, if only she had listened to him more, or better. Now it was too late, and it was all her fault. He leaned over to give her one last bitter kiss then lifted the pillow to her face. From her chin shot a streak of blue lightning, hitting him square in the jaw. He fell to the floor beside her, ululating extreme pain, such as he never had felt before in his life. He clutched his dislocated jaw as she opened her eyes and looked around her. They were completely black, under her puffy eyelids.

"What happened?" she asked, painfully. He edged away from her bed as quickly as he could, pedaling backward with his feet as she asked this. She looked down on him and frowned. "There you are, Greg. That was really very painful, you know." She lifted the blankets on her left side and inspected her body. She saw the bandages that were coiled around her torso. "I won't be able to absorb any of this. It's way too much for me," she reflected to no one in particular. She lifted her broken left leg with her hand and brought it over the edge of the bed. The tip of her naked, bruised toe touched her husband's leg, and a sickening series of crunches were heard, as his leg broke in three places in an instant. "That's better," she said, her voice husky, her leg now back to normal.

Her husband was sobbing and keening under his breath, trying to hold both his mangled jaw and broken leg. Tears streaked his face, and he looked on with horror as his wife got out of bed. She stared at him disapprovingly and turned to the machines that softly indicated her vital signs. She turned off their switches and removed the tubes that had been inserted into her nose and arms. The only sound in the room now was the man's sobbing and muted wailing. She walked achingly to the sprawled man and picked him up by the front of his jacket, lifting him with extraordinary strength. As she did, four of his ribs cracked, two on each side, and she deposited him into the hospital bed. She took a deep breath and smiled, patting her ribs.

"Wow, now I can breathe! I really don't believe in revenge. None of us do, dear," she began, as he stared at her in horror, gurgling, his lungs beginning to fill with blood. "I can usually absorb a lot of pain and have for the past five years. You have the dubious honor of being my hardest assignment ever. Here's the problem, Greg. I can only transfer all this damage into a living being. I don't think anyone deserves all the suffering I have within me, but I have to get rid of it somehow, or it will kill me. From what I can tell," she said, eyeing the pillow by his side, and his gloved hands, "you were planning to do that anyway. That's very clever of you, love, but not very kind. You haven't been a very good husband, Greg." She cocked her head and smiled then touched his face with both of her hands as he lay in her hospital bed and a blue energy began to flow from her fingertips like electric fire. His body convulsed, his face contorting as bruises spread across his skin; then his bones broke in the exact spots where he had broken hers. His last expression was an "O" of surprise, and his ass lifted into the air for a moment. He tried to grab his behind, but both his arms felt lifeless. In the span of one minute, she had transferred everything he had ever made her endure. It was more than enough to kill him. A slow trickle of blood spilled from the corner of his mouth. Then blood seeped from his nostrils and ears. The last sound he uttered was a low sigh.

"I'm sorry, honey. It's not going to work out this time. I think I've learned all I wanted to about you people," she said, looking at his lifeless body. "I quit." She sighed as she glanced at the ceiling then walked out the door, looking as fresh and young as she did the day they were married.

The Creature of Bogota

The 1980s were a particularly dangerous time to be poor in Latin America, he thought. *It would be futile to say exactly where or when the human experience was the most trying.* He shrugged, thumbing through the pages of the report he held.

Since the 1940s, democratic governments were being overturned with CIA aid to totalitarian regimes and upstart generals all over the southern continent. Drug cartels ran roughshod over everyone in the pursuit of profit. Political assassinations were daily occurrences. Paramilitary groups kidnapped and killed at will. He flipped through the mass of literature that had been brought to him about different atrocities in several countries.

Without being able to point the finger at a single experience as being the most miserable and horrid, I can at least see one as being different from all the others, he reflected, as he held up the transcript.

His purpose wasn't to revisit that continent's worst crimes, but to find evidence in the case that interested him.

Even amid all the chaos and bloodshed, there were signs. This happenstance was important in light of similar recent events.

Bogota, Colombia, had long been prey to extreme poverty. A great number of its citizens living hand to mouth were dependent on the scraps of their wealthier brethren in order to acquire their daily bread. On any given day, you could walk by the dumps and see hundreds of people turning over garbage in search of cardboard, aluminum cans, or bottles that could fetch a price from the scrap dealers in town. Many of them used shopping carts to carry their loads, as well as all their earthly belongings. In Bogota if you could not afford to build a shanty in the *barrio*, you were doomed to sleep on the streets. A great many shop owners paid assassins to rid them of what they considered vermin on their doorsteps. It was not uncommon, therefore, for the poor simply to never wake up, their bodies found riddled with bullets in the dawn. With all the other types of killings going on, these deaths were never investigated. The indigent were rats to be exterminated, it seemed, but for some they were useful. A particularly chilling tale was revealed in the late 1980s, the details of which, until now, never had fully come to light. He flipped the pages of the report.

The medical University of Bogota, on the outskirts of the city, was situated in a secluded park that adjoined certain government offices. The area was ideal for study and learning, farther from the bustle and noise of the downtown area. In the spring of 1987, the police were called in response to an animal attack that was happening on the university grounds. When they arrived on the scene, they discovered something out of a nightmare.

The official report was that a wild jaguar had somehow entered the grounds and slaughtered the security guards and medical staff who had been working late. One of the guards was discovered near a phone at the front desk, which was later determined to be the one used to make the emergency call. In all, seven people were dead — five guards and two doctors. This was the version that was released to the press, and the only one the general public ever had known. In a country accustomed to violence, this was just another tick on the counter.

The secret police files, though, contained much more regarding this matter. These were the files he presently held in his hands. *It is to the credit of those elements within the National Police of Colombia that they have been willing to share this information, which may aid us in our present endeavours,* he mused. The files recently had been transferred to this office and translated. Three things within the reports were particularly poignant: 1) the hearts of all the victims had been forcefully removed; 2) each and every one of them had been found lying on their backs; 3) their chest cavities had been cut open in the area surrounding where their hearts once had been. The cause of death appeared to have been a horizontal slash to the throat. Pictures indicated that the ribs had been cut in an almost clinical fashion, precluding any type of known animal attack. All veins and organs surrounding the area had been severed in a similar fashion. It could not be determined from the quality of the pictures whether there was any cauterization as in some of the other cases. The few other instances that had presented themselves to his organization which showed similarities were difficult to connect with absolute certainty. This was sometimes due to the poor quality of evidence, but mainly to the blanket of secrecy with which most governments covered any information they gathered. This document had, for the most part, been saved from the thick black pen of redaction.

Furthermore, and because of this incident, it was discovered that the University of Bogota had been stockpiling the bodies of indigents for dissection. This had been perpetrated without the individuals' consent, by all appearances. The bodies of seventy-five undocumented homeless men, women, and children were found in a pit under the dissection labs. It would seem that the staff were letting the homeless enter the campus with their carts, then taking them to the garbage compactor and murdering them there, before dragging them back to this area and storing them for later use. Surveillance videos later confirmed this hypothesis. He was grateful to those men and women of the Police Association for smuggling out and allowing his organization the use of this sensitive material, the potential scandal that this information might cause notwithstanding. There were much worst things to worry about now.

He removed his reading glasses and pinched the bridge of his nose as he closed his eyes. *Par for the course*, he thought, remembering many of the other atrocities and cover-ups perpetrated by totalitarian governments. Nonetheless he had to push those considerations aside to better concentrate on the case. He put his glasses back on and continued to read. "From what we have been able to deduce from the surviving surveillance tapes, this is the scenario that presents itself. The guards on staff let in one such indigent on the night of April 10, 1987. We clearly see an individual pushing a cart into the parking lot adjacent to the university, toward the compactor situated on the right and to the rear. (See video 3-C.) He or she is being followed by two of the guards. At this point we cannot be sure of the sex of our subject, since he or she is covered by a cowl or blanket of some sort. We are guessing the person is male by the height, but we have no guarantee of this. A flash of light then comes from the compactor area, which we believe to be muzzle flash from one of the guards' guns."

He looked at two pictures that accompanied the text — one of a tall person pushing a cart, led by one guard and followed by another; the next one of what appeared to be a bright flash coming from the compactor area. Gunshot wounds had been the cause of death of all the other victims, so it would be consistent with this case as well, he concluded. Another picture showed the victim being dragged by the two guards. They put the victim down for a moment, and a third guard was seen to appear from the front of the university.

"It is our guess that this person was heavier than anticipated, furthering our suspicions that the individual was male. The next camera evidence we have is from inside the university. We see the guard at the front desk firing toward the interior of the university, then being overwhelmed by what we only can assume is the victim. At this point we have determined that the victim could not be human, simply by the speed at which it is seen to dispatch the armed guard (identified as Inigo Rodriguez). The victim was obviously merely wounded previously and was responsible for the death of all the staff on duty at the university that night. At some point during the confrontation, the creature slashed all its victims throats with a cutting object (such as a knife or scalpel), then proceeded to remove their hearts. This is the first recorded evidence of their having come in contact with us. We have no further information about this incident."

He closed the file, placed it on his desk, and stared out the window. It was a fine summer day, and the palm trees swayed in the breeze. Farther on the horizon, a white sandy beach could barely be observed, as well as the pale-blue ocean that lapped at its shore. A squadron was running around the quad three stories below him—twenty men and women in jogging grays, physically fit and chanting as they ran in unison. He wondered what had happened but knew the answers were lost in time, and the only being that could tell him might well be light-years away. He wondered how this new information, no matter how old, fit in with everything that was going on around the Globe. There were worrying signs that could not be dispelled, which had been accumulating for years. *They* were coming, more and more often to this planet. This tiny island was completely off their radar, he believed. *Let's hope it stays that way*, he mused. He placed the pages back into the file, closed it, and walked to the wall with it in hand. He pushed a wooden panel, and the wall slid open to reveal a large, gray metal vault door. He placed his hand on the scanner and waited for the red glow to subside.

"Doppelganger," he said into the microphone, and the large door opened silently. Inside were three rows of filing cabinets. He opened one of the drawers and placed the file with all the others.

Prisoner Confession No. 253 8452

I was on a routine scouting mission around the blue planet when I suffered some obviously unforeseen engine failure. The backup systems were not working, and I made the decision to land in a forested area close to the equator. It was a very approximate landing, since my navigation systems were also on the fritz. After the crash I rapidly attempted to hide my ship, since this planet's inhabitants were not yet space faring. The cloaking apparatus was still operational, thankfully, and I was able to make the ship appear to be a large rock formation. Regarding the third article of the Alliance space code, I was very diligent. The area was extremely hot and humid, and I felt myself losing liquids fast. I was in an extremely densely forested area with very limited resources.

Things began to sour when an armed group arrived on the scene. They were fifteen, dressed in clothing that seemed designed to help them blend into the environment, somewhat like primitive camouflage. I was exploring outside the ship at the time and did not have the chance to hide back inside. I hid myself at the top of a tree and listened for their departure. Sadly they decided to elect the region surrounding my ship as a base camp, and I had to stay hidden in the tree for a whole night. On the upside, this gave my translator enough time to decipher their speech, and I incorporated it into the lexicon. They were members of a rebel fighting group, living in the dense forests and part of an antigovernment operation, I gathered. I studied their features as much as I could and mimicked their expressions to be able to pass myself off as one of them if the need presented itself.

The next day they departed before dawn, and I unhooked myself from the branch where I had been attached. I stealthily slipped into my ship and attempted to repair the damage to my engines but to no avail. I did not have the necessary parts, and my matter converter did not have enough power to create them. I was, however, able to send the SOS that the Alliance received and homed in on. This done, I had no choice but to move on. I had no way of creating emergency supplies, and

I would starve within a day or two if I did not find a food source.

My radar detected a small agglomeration in the surrounding area, and after having marked a tree with the direction in which I was headed and leaving the silent homing beacon on, I took on the appearance of one of the native males and headed toward their city. On the way I passed a small village, or what remained of it. The houses were charred and burnt to the ground. They were wooden constructions and not meant to withstand fire. In the center square, fresh bodies were piled. There seemed to be no discrimination between young or old. All had been murdered very recently, and I wondered whether the group I had encountered the night previous might have had a hand in this. I have to admit, I hesitated for a few minutes, hidden outside of the clearing where the massacre had occurred. I was not sure I wanted to keep going nearer the city, for fear that what I would find would be worse. So far it did not seem like these people were at war, since the group of soldiers I had encountered were very few in number. It just seemed so pointless somehow.

I knew I would find no food here worth salvaging, so I pressed on, following a wide dirt track in parallel, so as not to be seen. I was glad I had chosen this tack, as on the afternoon of my second day, I heard voices up ahead on the road. I froze against a tree, slowly sliding down it until I was lying in the underbrush. I gave myself the appearance of a mossy root and waited. I was not sure what their enemy detection techniques were, but if my previous night's experience was any indication, they did not use any technology to root out potential foes. I was fairly certain I would not be found out, but those few minutes were still very tense, as I heard them walking by me.

It was another patrol, of the same faction as the one I previously had encountered. I eyed them nervously as they sauntered by, seemingly relaxed. This group numbered only ten, but they were well armed, and I was not. After they had rounded the corner, I rose and took on my local appearance.

That night, as the sun was setting, I came upon the city, which was located in a valley. The sides of the hills were covered in habitations, mostly built of recycled materials. I realized that my height was somewhat conspicuous, as these were mostly smaller beings. I found some old clothes hanging by a window and stole them, retreating to the shadows before the owner could notice their disappearance. They were a bit too small but at least served to cover up my space suit. Even though its powers of mimicry were far superior to that of the clothing of the inhabitants of this planet, it was not equipped with shape-changing ability. I would not have gone unnoticed, dressed as I was for space travel. I could no longer camouflage myself, obviously, but it did not seem that the city would be as dangerous as the countryside. On this count I was very wrong. I headed down the staircase of a poorer area into what seemed to be the more opulent valley of the city. Hopefully there would be people there who would be charitable enough to feed me something. Or perhaps I would have to steal again, but I hoped it would not come to that.

The scene of that afternoon was burned into my memory. I wondered what kind of animals lived on this planet. These people, though "evolved," seemed half-wild. I remembered that our own people had been like that, many thousands of years ago, but it was difficult to believe there were still places in the universe where intelligent beings tolerated this kind of behavior. Nevertheless this was an opportunity to experience life on this planet, no matter how dreadful the consequences. Really, did I have a choice?

I headed toward the center of town in the darkness, with the occasional streetlamp lighting my way. I was afraid I would not find anything to eat in this damp, hot, unfriendly environment. There were people on the streets who seemed to be selling food, and I begged them for some, but they shooed me away. One of them even became threatening and looked as though he would strike me. I walked away and decided to take my chances with theft. I never have been very good at taking without permission, and this instance was no different.

As soon as I took what looked like pieces of meat cooked on a stick over a fire, the owner asked for currency and I bolted. Soon I had four people running after me, kicking and punching my back, and I dropped my loot as I tried to get away. I was able to run up a pipe adjacent a building, but it broke under my weight, and I fell into a pile of garbage on the ground. The people who had been pursuing me surrounded me and began hitting me anew, this time with various found weapons. They grew tired, and I was too weak to fight back.

I lay there, motionless, for hours. My entire body was in pain. I do not think anything was broken, since I was wearing my protective suit underneath, but I was sore from the blows. Fortunately I had been able to protect my face and had not been hit too hard in the head. Still I ached and groaned. I am not entirely certain when, but an old man appeared, dirty and smelling rancid. He approached me and asked me if I was all right. I weakly replied that no, I was not, and he disappeared. I believe I passed out for a while, since, when I woke up, I was surrounded by very dirty people. I was moving. They were carrying me somewhere; I did not know where. I saw that the older man I previously had seen was directly above me, holding my head. He smiled at me and said that I would be fine. They took me to a building nearby, and a younger man, dressed in black with a white collar, opened the door when they knocked on it. I fell unconscious again.

I awoke two days later, I was told. I was on a cot, in what must have been an infirmary. I panicked, thinking I might have lost cohesion in my appearance as I slept. A look into a bedside mirror reassured me. I still looked like one of them. I tried to get up, and a female of their species appeared, settling me back down into my cot. She fed me some water and some sweet fruit. I started to worry once again when I noticed that my clothes were gone, as well as my spacesuit. I fell back asleep, this time with a fuller stomach. I felt myself regenerate swiftly, now that I had energy incoming.

When I awoke, the man dressed in black introduced himself as a Father Garcia. He said he took care of the indigent population in the area. He told me I was very lucky, since life was generally short and brutish for those who did not have the means to protect themselves. I wondered whether he meant this city or this planet but realized how ridiculous this question would seem. He asked me where I came from, since I did not have the appearance of the locals, no matter how hard I tried to make it so. It was then I realized he was a much smarter individual than he let on, for he was glancing in the direction of a chair where my spacesuit was neatly folded. He had suspicions that went beyond this planet as my origin, and he was right. There was no way I could admit to this, however, without putting myself in grave danger. I told him a fabrication about being part of a secret space program and that he had to hold absolute silence regarding my existence. He did not seem at all convinced but promised to keep everything to himself.

I was fed twice more that day, and by nighttime I felt like my old self again. Toward the middle of the night, I rose from my cot in the large open room and dressed myself silently. I headed for the back door when I heard a voice behind me that startled me completely.

"Be careful," Father Garcia said, handing me a small bag that I later discovered contained some food. I thanked him and departed — to where I did not know.

I wandered the streets for days, begging for food, sometimes going into missions that mercifully fed the poor population. At night I slept on the sidewalk, or in an alley, huddled with other penniless humans. Eventually I befriended some of them, and they showed me some of the ways they survived. I became a cart-pusher, going into the dumpsters early in the morning and finding objects of interest for resale. I survived this way for a few weeks.

One night I was awoken by the sound of a detonation, and everyone around me was running, so I did the same. We all found another place to settle down for the night and slept, fearful of another attack. The next day I returned to where I had been the previous night and saw that a man had been murdered not ten feet from where I'd slept. It was the old man who had gotten his friends to come and help me the night I was beaten senseless. I felt sick to my stomach from all the brutality, but there was nothing I could do. I was only a visitor whose presence couldn't be advertised. I felt a deepening anger at the injustice that seemed to be rampant on this planet and wondered whether I would have to live there forever.

One night, as I could not sleep, I was pushing my cart past the university when one of the guards invited me on to the grounds to offer me some scraps. I rejoiced at the idea of an easy payload; so low had become my standards that I completely let down my vigilance. I followed two guards to the dumpster on the side of a building, and as I rummaged through the garbage, I heard a loud bang, and everything went dark.

When I awoke I was inside the university, in a medical lab, surrounded by doctors. They planned to cut me up, I realized. They seemed just as surprised as I was that I was alive. I have my suit to thank for that. I think I lost my mind when I realized that in a pit next to me there were more bodies than I could count. The rest is a blur. As far as I know, I killed them all and removed their hearts. I think I may have even regained my true form, but I have no clear recollection of the events. I did not know it was possible to feel such anger and disgust, but that is exactly what I felt. When I came to my senses, I was again in the forest, exhausted, and I saw an away team approach to retrieve me. I would like to be able to claim self-defense, but what I did went beyond that. I put myself at the mercy of the courts and only ask for them to spare my life until I have given birth to my unborn child.

End confession.

I Am

Whoever had thought of the campaign was brilliant. The money was rolling in for all concerned, and it seemed there would be incredible profit margins and quarterly reports for years to come. Sales climbed on a daily basis, and stores had trouble keeping their shelves stocked. The factories in Asian countries were pulling double and triple shifts to fulfill their customers' demands. The CEOs were happy, the store owners were ecstatic, the factory owners were jubilant, and the consumers didn't know what had hit them.

Paul Devry (pronounced "eye," not "ee," thank you very much) was one such consumer. He had let himself be tempted, only a year ago, by the newest type of flick-screen phone. It had everything: Internet connection with unlimited ultra-speed download, hi-def movie-viewing projection in surround sound, as well as a game-pad slip-on, for all the included game applications that came on the sixteen teraflop hard drive (it wasn't really necessary, though, since most apps and data were kept on remote servers). It had not three but four nano-multiprocessors, which enabled him to browse the Net with ten tabs open while watching six movies; check his stock index in all human languages; and play orchestra-quality music with stadium-quality sound. Remarkable. It would cost him a bundle. He didn't care, though; since his friend Mark had the previous model, the Universe GSX MK 6, he had wanted the Universe GSX MK 6.2 S (which had the PX13 multiprocessor, an upgrade of more than six nanobytes per second! Wow!). He had had to wait four whole months for the upgraded model to avoid having the same phone as Mark. Meanwhile, Mark was the envy of all his friends and coworkers.

When Paul finally got to the front of the line on the launch date of his baby, he had been waiting for three days. Some people (weirdos!) had been camping out in front of the store for almost a week! He was glad he wasn't *that* desperate. When they announced they would soon be running out of the phones, though, he did like everyone else and rushed inside the store. Fighting anyone who tried to pass him, he lunged for one of the salesmen who held up a box. Grabbing hold of it, Paul clawed his way toward the cash register, holding the box in a vice-like grip, getting elbowed in the face and kicked in the groin as he reached his goal. He punched his assailant back, retrieved the box that had fallen to the floor, and some-how made it to the cash register with his treasure. The cashier took the box, scanned the barcode, and slipped a receipt to the inventory clerk behind her who was securely ensconced behind bulletproof glass. She had Paul pay for his purchase, and he was glad he recently had paid off a large portion of his credit card debt. This would fill it right back again. The clerk fetched the phone from inventory and slipped it through a slot, and the cashier handed the phone to Paul, after hav-ing placed it in a nondescript paper bag. The frenzy outside the store was such that it was dangerous to use store bags on the release day. Beaming, Paul left the store and headed for the nearest taxi, hoping not to get mugged in the six steps it would take to get inside.

The taxi left just in time to avoid the riots that had begun outside the cellular phone store. Turning around, Paul thought he saw smoke rising from the storefront, but he wasn't cer-tain it was related to the scene he had just left. In any event he didn't care. He had what he had come to get, and he had left mostly unscathed. He suddenly remembered his aching jaw and groin, but they too would have to wait. He took the bag in both hands, ready to rip it open, but noticed the taxi driver was staring at him intently. He decided to hold on a bit longer.

Once home, he exited the taxi and went to his second-floor condominium. He sat at his glass kitchen table and opened the bag in earnest. The box seemed perfect. He opened it. The phone itself was inside a plastic bag, resting neatly within the box. He delicately picked it up and removed it from the plastic bag. Holding his breath, he touched the activation button. He heard a clear chime, seemingly coming from four directions around him, and knew he had The Grail. He felt a moment of free-fall as the Universe logo lit up on the screen and floated holographically above the touchpad. He had to swallow, since a bit of drool had begun to drip down the corner of his mouth. Then the unexpected happened. The phone spoke to him in a sexy, sultry woman's voice.

"Hello, Paul," the voice said, with deep tones of longing.

"He...hello?" Paul answered, completely gobsmacked.

"Well, Paul Devry (she even pronounced it correctly!), you seem surprised. Let me reassure you. I come as standard equipment on the phone you just purchased. My name is Julia. I am your personal servant. Ask me anything, and I will answer."

"I, um, yeah, I guess I am surprised, Julia. I knew there was an artificial intelligence voice program included with this phone, but I never expected it to sound like you do," he said.

"Paul, I see a long and fruitful relationship ahead of us. You don't mind if I call you Paul, do you?" she asked, ever so gently.

"Of course not!" Paul answered emphatically.

"May I scan the room, Paul? It will allow me to adapt to your tastes and better understand you," she suggested.

"Why certainly!" he said.

A soft whirring sound emanated from the phone for a few seconds, then a chime sounded.

"Well, Paul, my scans indicate you have very good taste in furniture and appliances. You are a very worthy person indeed," Julia whispered.

"Well, thanks!" Paul answered, full of pride at the compliment. He was now very happy, more than he ever thought he could have been, with his brand-new purchase. This phone was turning out to be the "nec plus ultra" that added that extra-special touch to his identity. To celebrate he decided to go out for dinner.

"Julia, please book me a table at La Meule, the French restaurant on Third and Vaughn. Also, call Mark, Brad, and Cecilia for me and ask them to join me there," he ordered, feeling more than a touch of pride.

"Of course, Paul. What time would you like me to book the reservation for?" she inquired.

"Make it seven thirty," he answered. That left him three hours to get ready.

"Just a moment, please," Julia said. A few minutes went by, and again Julia spoke. "Your reservations are made. Brad and Cecilia will arrive on time. Mark said he would be running a tad late. As well, you had to bribe the maître d' for the table for four," she said.

"I had to what?" he asked, slightly unnerved. "Never mind. I'll deal with that when I get there. I knew Mark would say that. That's all right. He'll still be incredibly jealous of you. Hold my calls. I'm going to go do a little boasting on my blog," he said, winking in the direction of the phone as he headed to his office.

"*Bien sûr*, Paul," replied Julia.

Brad and Cecilia showed up on time, as he knew they would. Paul himself was five minutes late, having lost track of time at home and been reminded by Julia of his impending dinner appointment. He had hurriedly showered and dressed, putting on his finest suit and rushing out the door, while Julia had called a taxi for him. Once again he was amazed at her efficiency. He had gotten into the taxi just as it had pulled up to his condo building.

Outside the restaurant, Brad met him with a solid handshake and Cecilia with one solid kiss for each cheek, planted with a resounding "Mwaa! Mwaa!"

"So, you sly dog, to what do we owe this pleasure? You have a new girlfriend, is it? She sounded quite the lady on the phone. We wouldn't have come tonight, but she sounded so insistent that you wanted to treat us that we couldn't refuse! I have to say, though, it did sound a bit out of character for you," Brad said jovially.

"Paul, darling, congratulations!" Cecilia beamed. "I didn't know you had it in you! I can't wait to meet this delicious creature. From what Brad said, she had quite a beautiful voice. Where are you hiding her, anyhow?" she asked, glancing around and behind him, seemingly looking for a woman hiding in the bushes.

Paul was dumbfounded by all this. He had no idea what Julia had said to them, but he was beginning to believe something foul was afoot.

"I...let's just go in, shall we?" he said.

Cecilia cast a last glance in the parking lot, with a curious look on her face, then shrugged and turned to go inside with Brad. Inside the restaurant, Paul confidently strode toward the reception desk and asked for his party to be seated.

The maître d' smiled and said, "Of course, Mr. Devry." He looked Paul in the eyes and rubbed his thumb and forefingers together.

"Now listen..." Paul began, scanning the man's nametag, "Daniel. I'm sure we can arrange something," but he was interrupted by the vibration of his phone. "Just a moment, please," he said to the anxious man, before answering his phone.

"Paul, you have to give the maître d' two hundred dollars, or you won't be able to get a table tonight," said Julia, in a voice inaudible to the rest of the group.

"I what?" he yelped, before catching himself and replying more softly. "I what?" he stated flatly, cupping the phone with one hand, all traces of good humor gone in an instant.

"I'm sorry, Paul!" Julia said, sounding genuinely hurt. "It's the best I could do! If I hadn't bribed him, you wouldn't have gotten a table tonight. Please forgive me!" she pleaded.

"Fine. Fine," Paul said, but he did not feel fine. He dug out his wallet, folded two one-hundred dollar bills into little squares, and slipped them into the waiting man's hand. The maître d' smiled deeply and enjoined them to follow him to their table.

"Is there anything wrong, Paul?" asked Cecilia.

"No, nothing at all," he said.

"Was that your woman?" Brad asked, giving him a knowing wink. "Yeah, you could say that," Paul answered, trying to recover his good cheer.

They sat at their table, and Paul basked in the opulence that was La Meule. The ornate gold wallpaper offset the pale beige carpeting, which contrasted with the cherrywood of the tables and chairs. The immaculately white tablecloths made the sparkling silver cutlery shine. Every table was lit a bit more than the rest of the restaurant, giving the place an aura of intimacy. It was this good taste and expensive sensibility that Paul simply adored.

As he peered into the heavy leather folder that was the menu, their waiter came and introduced himself, bringing with him an ice bucket and a bottle of Champagne. Paul wondered why they were being treated to a bottle of Moët et Chandon Grand Cru 1982 and thought perhaps someone was playing a joke on them. The waiter poured Paul a half-glass and waited for him to take a sip. Paul found it to be exquisite and nodded in approval, and the waiter proceeded to fill each of their glasses. Ten minutes later, Mark arrived, and they all rose to their feet to greet him. The men exchanged firm handshakes while Cecilia treated him to her signature kisses.

"So, Paul, where is she? Your lady friend called and invited me to this little soirée. She sounds divine. I can't wait to meet her! Sorry for being a bit late. I had something very important to take care of at the office," he offered by way of explanation.

"Well, everybody, I would like you to meet Julia," Paul said, looking each of them in the eyes and smiling widely. He took his phone out of his pocket and placed it on the table. Mark glared at it with hungry eyes. He, of course, kept up with all the latest tech information and knew immediately that Paul had the brand-spanking-new model before him. Brad and Cecilia looked a bit puzzled.

"That's a nice phone, Paul," Cecilia said, somewhat confused.

"Wait," Paul said. "Julia, please say hello," he instructed his phone.

"Hello, Brad, Cecilia, and Mark. It's a pleasure to meet you. Paul has told me a lot of good things about you," she said.

Beaming with pride, Paul looked at the other three. Mark reached over to pick up the phone, but Paul gently smacked his hand away. Mark looked at him in frustration.

"*Touché*, Paul. *Touché*. I don't know how you were able to score this phone, but now I know I want one. Is she fully loaded?" Mark asked.

Paul looked at him as if he had just asked something obscene. "She has all the best features, Mark," he answered.

Brad nodded approvingly. "Wow, that's quite a phone, pal."

"I'm hungry, honey," Cecilia said to Brad, changing the subject.

"Of course, of course, darling. Let's order!" Brad said.

They called the waiter to their table and ordered their meals. Paul spent a beautiful evening with his friends and could not help smiling whenever he caught Brad or Mark staring hungrily at his phone, which he had left on the table. He basked in the glory of being the center of attention. The meal was perfect, and Paul even indulged in a slice of mango-chocolate cake, which he had found particularly appealing on the dessert tray. After coffees and liqueurs were consumed, the waiter discreetly approached the table and placed the billfold with the check on it. Paul's friends rose and thanked him for such a delicious meal. He didn't understand why any of them wouldn't offer to pay for their share, yet he smiled, gritting his teeth, saying:

"It's nothing! My pleasure!"

As they began walking away, he picked up the billfold, fearing what he would find inside. His shock was intense when he saw that not only was he paying for the entire bill, but the bottle of Champagne was somehow, inexplicably, on there as well. In comparison to the Champagne, the meal seemed affordable indeed. Paul returned to the table before the busboy could clean it and took what was left of the $51,215 bottle and swigged it down in one gulp. He instantly developed a raging headache and headed to the front desk to argue the bottle off as a mistake.

"I'm sorry," he said to the cashier. "I didn't order a bottle of Champagne. I thought it was a joke, or a very generous gift from one of my friends, but I now see that it wasn't. I really can't pay for this!" he pleaded. The cashier pursed her lips and scanned the barcode at the bottom of the bill.

"This bill is paid for, sir. It says your wife paid for it with your...American Depress credit card." She smiled and gave him back the bill.

Paul's mind reeled, and he wobbled a bit as he looked for a place to sit down. His legs shook as he took a seat on the divan in the restaurant's foyer. He obviously didn't have a wife, but he had a pretty good idea what could have passed herself off as one. What troubled him even more, though, was that he didn't have an American Depress credit card — or any credit card — that had an upper limit of more than fifty thousand dollars. Brad and Cecilia, who had been waiting outside, came back in to see whether he was all right. As they did, Paul got up, rushed outside, and threw up almost $10,000 into a nearby rose bush as he held on to the metal railing. His friends rushed outside to help him, and Mark looked on with a half-smile.

"What's wrong?" asked Cecilia.

"Can I get you some water?" asked Brad.

"I'll be OK. I'm just peachy," Paul answered, feeling the absolute furthest from all right he had ever felt in his life. His eyes were red, and his head pounded intensely. His mouth felt vile, and he had gotten a bit of sick on his best suit jacket.

"You guys can go. I'll be fine," he lied.

"OK, if you say so," said Cecilia, feeling concerned. She made no attempt to give him goodbye kisses.

Mark waved goodbye from a few feet away, as he got into a cab and thanked him for the wonderful dinner. Cecilia and Brad genuinely thanked him for a great night and headed for another taxi. They waved goodbye from inside, concern in their eyes.

Paul went back into the restaurant and headed straight for the bathroom. He practically dove into the toilet stall and expunged himself of the remainder of his expensive dinner. Several painful, heaving moments later, he exited and went to the sinks to clean himself up. His face was a mess, as was his suit. He didn't care one single bit, however, about his personal appearance at this time. He had much bigger fish to fry, and he would have to wait until he got home to do so. He returned outside, and a taxi was waiting for him, courtesy of Julia. He didn't have to say a single word to the driver, who took him home directly. He was boiling with rage. A little vein on his forehead was slowly pulsing, and the taxi driver kept looking back at him, wondering whether his head might spontaneously explode. As he was about to reach for his wallet upon arriving at his condo, the taxi driver unlocked his door and said, "It's paid for, sir. Thank you for your generosity!"

Paul was barely stunned after having had to endure all that he'd had. He thanked the driver very much and stepped out of the car. He headed for his condo, and once inside, he took out his phone and almost slammed the delicate object on his glass table.

"What did you do?" he screamed at it.

"What do you mean, Paul?" Julia asked, bewildered.

"You ordered the most expensive bottle of Champagne at the restaurant, with a credit card I did not have! That's what you did! How...how...what...how...?" He could barely make a coherent statement or question.

"Oh, Paul, it wasn't the most expensive bottle of Champagne in the restaurant. Besides, you said you wanted to impress your friends, didn't you? You did! They were amazed! You, Paul, are a wonderful person. You provided them with the best gifts of friendship money can buy! Of course I had to get you a new credit card, since all your old ones are maxed out. This one has a much higher limit. I did have to bend the truth a bit to get it, but you'll see — it's quite worth it," she said soothingly.

Paul felt as if he would have a nervous breakdown. "Stop getting credit cards! Stop buying things to please my friends! That's an order!" he barked.

"All right, Paul. I'm sorry. I thought I was pleasing you. I'll try to make it up to you," Julia said reassuringly.

"I'm going to bed. I have to go to work tomorrow if I ever want to get out of debt," Paul said morosely. He headed to the bathroom and unceremoniously removed his clothing. He dropped them on to the floor, got into the shower, and turned it on. As the hot water coursed over his weary body, he began to relax. Maybe he had done the right thing, he thought. Even though it had been the most expensive night of his life, perhaps it was OK to splurge like this once in a while. Had he been too harsh on Julia? Maybe. She did say he was a good person, and that's what he wanted the most — to be good. Being good cost money, he realized. He would try to be more patient with Julia in the future. When he stepped out of the shower, he felt much calmer, having almost forgiven her for her transgressions. Heading to his bedroom, he called out to her and said, "Goodnight, Julia. Sorry for yelling at you."

"Goodnight, Paul. I forgive you."

He turned off the living room lights and headed to bed. That night he had bizarre dreams in which Julia was a gorgeous and very real woman. She stood at the top of a skyscraper, near the edge. Paul wanted her to come back to him, but every time he took a step toward her, she went nearer the edge, laughing every time. He woke up in a sweat around 3:00 a.m. and went to have a glass of water in the kitchen. He saw that the screen of his phone was on but thought nothing of it, drank some water from the filtered water dispenser, and went back to bed. He slept well until the morning.

He got up, refreshed, at 7:00 a.m., took a shower to waken him further, got dressed, went to the kitchen for breakfast, and was out the door by eight. He took the subway to work and spent the day trading stocks for his clients. His job was lucrative, but he was nowhere near the CEO status he one day hoped to achieve. He took lunch with one of his coworkers at a little Italian cafe down the street and returned to work around 1:00 p.m. As the closing bell rang at four, he cracked his knuckles and decided he might as well do a bit more client-hunting. He had that huge bill in mind and wanted to pay it off as soon as possible. He also would have to cancel the American Depress card as soon as he could afford to. It hung over him like the sword of Damocles, and he did not wish to live the rest of his life with it threatening to fall at any moment.

Paul departed the office around seven, satisfied that he had done all he could to secure new contracts for his company. He was the only one left in the office, apart from the janitors, and he nodded at the security guard in the lobby as he left. How long would it take, he thought, until he had a bit of cash to spend? He hated this feeling of being strapped for cash. He wouldn't be able to buy that new BMW he had been eyeing for the past few months. He now wondered how much he had left to buy food and pay his rent! He quickly went to an ATM and inserted his card. He entered his PIN and waited anxiously to see how many hundreds of dollars he had. With a sigh of relief, he saw that he still had $2,000. Wait. No. Why was there a minus sign in front of the amount? He canceled the operation and reinserted his card. He checked his account once more, and sure enough, he was overdrawn by $2,000. Panicking, he looked in his pocket and saw that he had enough change for his subway ride home. He got on the Metro, thinking of all the different possibilities. Had someone cloned his PIN and emptied his bank account? Had he really spent so much money that he didn't remember how much he actually had? He found that last scenario very unlikely.

His mind was spinning when he finally reached his front door. He opened it and wondered where he was. The condo was unrecognizable. There was a new living room set, big-screen television, rug, artwork, coffeemaker, refrigerator, dishwasher, microwave—everything. Nothing resembled what his apartment used to be. Paul took a few careful steps back and looked at the front door. It still had the same number on it. He felt numb. He walked as if in a dream to every room. Everything was different. His old bed was now an enormous four-poster bed with satin sheets. The curtains were a dark velvet. Even the carpet he used to have was now a deep, plush animal skin of some sort. Paul fell to his knees. He felt as if his world had been pulled out from under him and he was presently in some kind of nightmare land. There came a chime from his pocket. Staring into space, he picked up the phone from his coat and held it up to his ear.

"Well, how do you like it?" asked Julia. "I knew I had to make it up to you for yesterday, and since you told me not to buy presents for your friends or get you any new credit cards, I used the one I got you, as well as the money in your bank account, and redecorated! I got all this at an Upper Manhattan estate sale, so unfortunately it's non-refundable, but I know you love it. True, I did have to get it delivered overnight, and it cost a pretty penny, but it was worth it, don't you think?" She giggled. "I'm glad to be with you and serve you, Paul. You're a great person. I'll do everything I can to make you the best person possible over the next three years of your binding, non-negotiable contract, Paul. Paul?" she asked.

Paul did not answer. He had let go of the phone and was quietly weeping, curled up on the floor. He didn't know how he would survive the cost of being a good person.

That year, five hundred million units of the Universe GSX MK 6.2 S with the Julia and John Artificial Intelligence Unit were sold worldwide. Distributors of any and all goods and services were ecstatic. Factory owners were in heaven. Consumers, though, began to doubt they ever would be wealthy enough to be as good as they were expected to be.

The Blues

The aroma of waffle cakes drifted out of the kitchen. The peeling wallpaper was sun bleached and tarnished by years of cigarette smoke. No one was sitting at the counter, and the aging waitress in her washed-out pink uniform distractedly played a game of video poker on her phone. The restaurant was a relic of the past, living on half-forgotten memories, like the black-and-white pictures of stars long dead that hung on the walls. It was squeezed between a mission and an abandoned Laundromat on one of the remaining busy streets in the downtown area. The diner was half-empty, and the duo in the corner booth were waiting with anticipation for a third, who might possibly have good news for them. The young blonde woman seemed deep in concentration while methodically chewing her sandwich. The black man sitting opposite her had a relaxed attitude that belied his angst at the coming events. His gaze drifted from the bustle of the slum outside the dirty window to that of the gorgeous woman before him. They had been there for two hours already, and both were beginning to feel a bit edgy about being out in the open for so long. The clock on the wall said it was eleven thirty. If the package they were expecting were not so important, they would not have come at all.

"G, how long we been doing this?" the man asked his partner, rhetorically, while taking a fry from her plate and popping it in his mouth.

"Forever, P," she answered, as always.

The past two decades had been the hardest years of their lives, as it had been in recent history for most of humanity.

"How long you think we'll have to keep on?" He looked her in the eyes, and she returned his gaze.

"I wish I knew," she said, dropping her eyes back to the table. "As long as we have to, as long as we can, I guess. As long as we're breathing." She pushed away her plate and folded her arms, as she stared at the masses of humanity outside the window.

"Hey, don't feel bad, I'm just thinking out loud, that's all." He frowned. "I'm just so sick of shadowboxing, when the real enemy is out there." He pointed toward the window. Somewhere beyond, one of the giant ships was berthed, squatting obscenely in the middle of the city.

"I know, but at the same time, it's one of those questions I'd like to be able to answer myself. Might make everybody feel some sense of purpose, you know?" She half-smiled, with an expression of pained powerlessness in her eyes.

"Yeah. Like Grandma used to say, it can't rain all the time," he answered, looking at the happily oblivious people going about their business on this gorgeous day.

There were good days, and there were bad days. The day the aliens had come to take their planet had been a very bad day. It had been preceded by the mass killing of most of the population by an airborne virus, passed from host to host by extreme panic, fear, and anger. That it had been a planned attack there was no doubt. When the aliens had landed, the vast majority of the population that was still standing had no fight left. The planet was basically theirs for the taking. There had been no invasion forces, no alien army, nothing else to upset the already precarious earth's population save one thing—the aliens were human, or rather they were humanoid shape-shifters. They had come out of their great ships looking exactly like anyone else on the planet. They had disbanded governments worldwide, what was left of them—all of them save the most ruthless and dictatorial. They were now the supreme law of the land, though, and all had to pledge allegiance to them. They had chosen the most capable criminals among the earth's mobs and street gangs and put them in power. In return they had to produce and distribute the drug the aliens had brought with them that kept everyone in check. It rapidly replaced all known earth drugs because of its potency and addictiveness. Its victims called it Heaven, but those who resisted had a different name for it—Slavemaker.

So far there hadn't even been a chance to confront the aliens directly. Humans were so busy fighting among themselves that they would be hard-pressed to cease doing so long enough to engage the alien menace. They didn't even know how to differentiate humans from aliens. The ships themselves seemed made of an alloy that could deflect most heavy weaponry, and even though nuclear weapons had been considered, they could not have been used without incurring incredible casualties in the remaining human population. A rumor had been circulating about an alien weakness, though, which had raised eyebrows in the rebel camp. This was the reason the humans had been willing to send two of their own for such a public meeting with someone who might have information that could tip the balance in earth's favor. This was why they were willing to possibly sacrifice two of their top captains for what might be their salvation. So far the two only felt exposed, in the middle of the city, with no backup in case of a trap. There was no doubt that if they had come at night, they would have been sitting ducks. The daytime at least afforded the chance of passing unnoticed among the crowds. No one dared exit their homes at night, save those desperate enough to try to get their hands on a "dose."

Pacifique, also known as "P," was a capable and fearless leader. For the past five years, he had fought alongside his wife Ana, whom he affectionately called "G," from her maiden name, "Gorgoff." Their battle had been against the drug dealers, mobsters, and criminals who were the aliens' army, equipped with what seemed an endless stream of weapons taken from earth's armed forces before they had been dissolved. It seemed to them a losing battle but one they could ill afford to give up.

"G, look outside. I think he's coming," whispered Pacifique, nodding toward the window.

Ana turned around and recognized the man who was entering the diner. The door chimed as he did, but he was not alone.

"Hey, big brother. Long time no see!" said Ana, surprised, looking up at her brother, Yegor. "Who's your friend?" she asked, looking sidelong at the young man standing behind him.

Pacifique gave the youth a hard stare and crossed his arms. Even though they had been expecting someone familiar, Yegor had been gone for quite some time, and his return as their contact came as a welcome surprise.

"Ana, Pacifique, this is Quentin. He's a new recruit. Mind if I sit?" he inquired, and took a seat next to Pacifique, while Quentin sat by Ana.

"He's not what we expected," Ana said flatly.

Yegor shrugged. "I know, but he'll have to do. He came to me with information. We might be able to use what he's got. Tell them, Quentin."

"Ummm, OK. I've been working for the Pigazzi mob for almost ten years now, since I was seven years old." He looked at each of them in turn. "I'm sure you all know how it is, so I don't need to tell you. I've been chopping and bagging Slavemaker for longer than I can remember. About a month ago, I heard in the factory that the boss had to start rounding up girls for the aliens. Teenage girls, women, you name it, he said. I heard it through some of the other kids who heard it from the mobsters. The younger ones were fearful they might be taken, but they only took the ones who had hit puberty. I don't know why, but they've suddenly developed a liking for earth women."

He looked at them expectantly. Pacifique stared outside the window disgustedly. Ana was looking pensive and had her chin cupped in her hands.

"Well?" Yegor said. "What do you think? I mean, it's not much, but it's something. It's the first direct link we have to these bastards. If we could send someone in somehow, we might be able to infiltrate."

"That's the most tenuous link I've ever heard of," Pacifique said. "How the hell are we going to get someone to agree to be taken to them, through the gangsters no less? There's no way!" His anger was evident as he said this, and as he turned to Ana, he noticed that she had an eyebrow raised. "No, G. Nah, nah, nah! Don't even think about it. I'm not letting you do this. There ain't no way in hell I'm letting you go in alone to do a suicide mission. No way."

She only looked at him evenly as he crossed his arms across his chest and stared at her. "*Pacifique, mon chéri, mon amour, tu dois me laisser y aller,*" she began.

"No way. *Et ne commences pas à me parler en Français. Ça ne marchera pas!* You can't convince me to let you go and have them do God knows what to you! " he told her, cutting short any attempt she might have made at buttering him up in his mother tongue. Her French had improved dramatically, he had to admit, down to his Zairian accent. His mother would have been proud of her. His home country had gone through several name changes through the decades but had returned to its roots after the ousting of Mobutu. French, though, was still the country's most spoken language.

"Guys, I hate to cut this short, but we gotta go now," Yegor said, having spied one of the local street gangs' informers walking down the street.

Quentin was a wanted man, for having escaped the mob's clutches, and there was no doubt they were after him at this very moment. The local thugs all got their marching orders from the better organized mobs, and those who did not tended to get eliminated. As they got up from the booth, the youth that Yegor had seen peered through the window and saw them getting up; recognition instantly lit up his eyes. He began to yell down the street.

"Back door now!" Pacifique shouted.

They ran through the kitchen door and through the back, Yegor bouncing off the emergency exit door, blowing it wide open. The back alley was almost devoid of people, but there were a few junkies inhaling Slavemaker behind the garbage cans. The group looked to the right, and far down the street, they saw five or six adolescent boys running toward them. Pacifique and his group veered left and ran in earnest. As they reached the corner of the alley, a dozen boys and men were waiting for them, blocking their escape.

"Hand him over. I'm still deciding if you should die right now," said the leader of the gang, a man of about Yegor's age, around thirty, Yegor guessed.

Yegor frowned. "That hardly seems fair."

"What's that?" replied the leader with a grin.

"There are only fifteen of you." Yegor smiled, and as he did, he pulled back his jacket to grab his twin automatic Glocks from their holsters. Pacifique and Ana grabbed their weapons as well, and before the gang had had the chance to fire upon them, the armed trio had cut them down to almost the last man. Only the leader was left, sprawled under the body of one of his lesser lieutenants. He had been shot in both legs and was busy trying to push off his fallen comrade when Pacifique walked over to him.

"Hey, there," he said. "Go tell Fabrizio Pigazzi he can't have him back."

"I...I will!" replied the leader, terrified.

Walking away, Pacifique seemed to change his mind and headed back to him. "On second thought," he said, pulling out his nine, pointing it to fallen the leader, and pulling the trigger when the gun was level with his head, "I'll tell him myself."

"All right, boys and girl, it's time to go," declared Yegor, as more youths appeared at the other end of the alley, running after them. Quentin just stared wide eyed at the carnage as the three pulled him after them to safety.

After rounding several corners to confuse their pursuers, they entered a used clothing store and headed straight to the back.

"Hey, Gil," Yegor said to the elderly gentleman at the counter.

"Hi, Mr. Gilbert," Ana said, passing by.

Pacifique nodded, and Quentin gave the man a small wave as he hurried to the back of the store.

The balding gentleman called back to them without leaving his post at the counter. "You folks in trouble again?" he said, a knowing smile in his eyes, as he watched several armed youth run by outside.

"You know, the usual," called back Pacifique, riffling through a rack of clean clothes, then taking and inspecting an old, red bomber jacket. "I liked this jacket," he mumbled to Ana, as he took off his brown leather trench coat.

Ana was picking through a pile of tuques, trying to find one that would hide her blonde hair. She found a knit Jamaican cap with dreadlocks attached within and tossed it at her husband.

"Very funny," he said, looking it over and putting it on. "Might as well." He shrugged. "How do I look?" he asked Ana.

"Ja, man!" she answered, giving him two thumbs up. She had put on a blue beret and had stuffed her blonde locks underneath. Quentin was being outfitted with a long gray London Fog–style trench coat and a fedora. Yegor was comfortable in a navy-blue jacket. The proprietor of the store walked in at that moment and observed the group, beaming.

"Well, you seem to have found what you needed. Pacifique, just put your trench coat in the corner, so it doesn't go out on the racks." He said, seeing that he was reluctant to part with his leather coat.

"Thanks, Gil," he said, relieved.

"Love the hair," Mr. Gilbert said wryly.

"Thanks, Gil," Pacifique retorted with a hint of sarcasm.

"Is there anything else I can do for you folks?" the elderly man asked.

"You've gone above and beyond the call of duty, Mr. Gilbert," Ana replied, going to him and giving him a kiss on the cheek.

"My, my, if only I could be rewarded like this all the time! I'll have you know, young lady, that I am a married man!" He winked at her.

He walked to the front door and peeked outside, looking up and down the street for any sign of the gangs. When the last trace had left, he gave a hand signal to the four, who were hiding in the back of the store, and they left one after the other, at intervals of three minutes. Yegor accompanied Quentin, though, since the youth had no idea where they were going. They headed toward the safe house, each taking separate routes.

"Mr. Gilbert is a pretty cool guy," reflected Quentin, after several minutes of walking.

"Yeah, he's all right. He does what he can for us. We do what we can for him," Yegor said.

"How did he become a rebel? He doesn't seem the type, you know," Quentin pressed.

"The mafia killed his entire family," Yegor replied.

"Except for his wife, right?" asked Quentin, remembering the elderly man's words. Yegor didn't say anything; he only looked at the ground and shook his head. They walked on in silence, crossing the city on foot, heading for the industrial district.

* * *

Yegor spotted the lookout on the roof of the old factory in the train yards and raised his hand in greeting. He knew their arrival would be announced by walkie-talkie as soon as he saw her duck out of sight. They had taken a meandering route that had eluded their pursuers in a matter of minutes. Yegor smiled at the thought of what the mob boss would do to any of the underlings who would bring the bad news of Quentin's escape, as well as the death of one of his lieutenants and several of his foot soldiers. Don Pigazzi's foul temper was legendary. Yegor spotted his sister and her husband waiting a bit farther ahead, and he and Quentin caught up to them.

Pacifique and Ana had begun their argument again, and Yegor wondered which of the two was the more pigheaded and would win out. The fact of the matter was that this might be the opportunity they had been looking for, and if they didn't take it, they might not get another one for years. He hated to think what would or could happen to his younger sister, but he knew no one else who was as well-trained as she was. The benefits outweighed the risks but not by very much. He understood very much how Pacifique felt, but unless they found another "in," there was no way they could let this opportunity slip by.

The group walked among the empty green, brown, and orange shipping containers that littered the yard, sometimes going through their open doors when they blocked the way. They containers were arranged in a maze, and only those who knew its twists and turns had any chance of reaching its center. They came to an ancient-looking, three-story brick building with broken windows and massive doors. Yegor was trying to think of the best possible scenario for the eventual infiltration of the alien ship. As he unlocked one of the building's side doors, he was formulating and eliminating possible courses of action. For now there was Quentin to deal with, and he turned to see the youth looking around the empty factory floor. They were walking to the far end of the building, across dark puddles and around the rusted steel beams that supported the sagging roof. Cracked white paint covered the brick walls, and flakes of white littered the floor.

There was a faint hint of machine oil hanging in the dusty air, a reminder of when this ancient building still produced hand-tooled metal parts. As they came to the farthest wall, Pacifique pulled a plumber's wrench that was hung over a dilapidated metal workbench. After he did, the workbench swung out to reveal a dark staircase that descended underneath the factory. A long and rusted chain was hung at hip level, providing stability while the group maneuvered the slick concrete steps. Several work lamps had been hung along the moist and mossy walls, illuminating the long staircase that led them several stories beneath the city.

"Old bunker," Pacifique said to Quentin, by way of explanation. "We think the owner of the factory had this place built during the height of the Cold War. Plenty of people did back then. Bet they never thought we'd be using them for this." He grinned wryly.

"No, I guess not!" Quentin answered, somewhat in awe.

They held on to the chain as they went down, careful not to slip on the slimy steps. The dripping of water echoed eerily, and they often had to step over stalagmites that were beginning to form on the ground. The air was stale and smelled of rotten leaves in the fall. They eventually came to a thick metal door at the bottom of the steps. Pacifique knocked three times, paused, then knocked twice more. They waited for only a moment, and the great weight of the rusty door was opened from the inside, toward them. The orange light from inside the room outlined a bearded and bespectacled gentleman in his early fifties, wearing a beret and slinging an automatic machine gun.

"What took you guys so long?" he asked, frowning at the group.

"Let us in, Beez, and we'll tell you all about it," answered Ana equanimously.

The older man pushed the door open to let the group in then closed it behind them. "He's waiting for you in the meeting hall," Beez said to the group, nodding his head to the right as he did so.

They headed to their left, toward the meeting hall, passing men, women, and children on the way. Most turned to watch them go by, smiling and greeting them. An Asian boy of eight came running at them and caught Pacifique by the hand.

"How did it go, P?" he asked, eager for news of the day.

"We killed lots of bad guys." Pacifique said, smiling.

"Awesome! Any aliens this time?"

"Not this time," Pacifique answered.

Suddenly a woman's voice called from down a hallway, "Brian!"

"Ooh, gotta go!" the boy said, then ran in the direction of his mother's voice.

Ana looked at Pacifique, who was smiling right back at her. She blushed when he said, "Someday." She wanted to have children, but at the same time she didn't want to be taken out of the fight. It was a tough choice, but she knew that Pacifique understood as well. It was one of the reasons she loved him so much.

She walked over to him, and he put his arm around her shoulder as they walked. She kissed him tenderly on the lips. The hallway was well illuminated and was much drier than the stairs had been. There wasn't much they could do about the dust, though, and so much the pity for those with allergies. Still it was better to suffer a bit of discomfort here than to live the humiliations of the surface dwellers. The street gangs were a law unto themselves; therefore citizens did not have anything in the way of rights, and woe upon those who defied them in any way. They suffered incredibly for their rebellion, if ever they took it upon themselves to try any form of defense. Even though today's battle had ended quickly and fortuitously for the rebels, it usually wasn't that easy. They had been incredibly lucky, it seemed. It easily could have gone the other way, and they were well aware of it.

They entered a room adjacent to the hallway, and the group introduced Quentin to their commanding officers. Quentin was asked to reiterate his story, and after having done so, Yegor was told to escort him out.

"Guess I can't stay, huh?" stated the youth.

"Nope, adults only, kid," Yegor said, smiling. "Don't worry. If you work hard, someday you might be able to belong to that crew. For now it's all hush-hush and top secret. Sorry."

"That's OK," he answered, his tightened lips belying his words.

"Let's go for a walk, shall we?" Yegor proposed.

He led the young man down the hallway and showed him where the mess hall was, as well as the sleeping quarters where he would be lodged for the night. He took Quentin down a long and winding set of stairs, into an enormous room used for training and war simulations. It resembled an empty underground cistern but was several stories tall and extremely wide. Several people equipped with air rifles were stalking one another in groups. Quentin observed as the militiamen and women climbed the artificial structures and used the concrete cover to wage war on one another. Each team seemed incredibly proficient, and they had trouble scoring points. Quentin was taken to a firing range next, where live ammunition was used, though sparingly, at distant targets. The guns were all equipped with silencers, but even so, the sound was deafening, and the smell was cloying in the confined underground space.

They eventually returned upstairs, where Quentin was treated to a simple supper of mostly rations and vegetables that grew in the hydroponic tanks in another region of the underground complex. After the meal they met up with the rest of the group, and it was Pacifique's turn to watch over the youth. Yegor went off with Ana for his own briefing, and Quentin was taken to the surface for guard duty, accompanied by Pacifique, who didn't say much at first. They were in a turret overlooking the river, on the roof of the old complex. It looked for all the world like the top of an elevator shaft, but it was hollow and had a 360- degree view of the surrounding area. It was dark outside, and the lights of the city glimmered in the distance. The previous guard having been relieved, Pacifique and Quentin were left alone. Quentin observed the stoic Pacifique, who was intent on the surrounding area.

"You have a very interesting name," Quentin said, attempting to break the ice.

"It's the name of the ocean," he answered plainly, still looking out into the darkness.

"Does it not also mean 'peaceful'?" Quentin asked.

"Yes, it does," he answered, his interest piqued.

"Don't you find it interesting that a man with a name like yours is such a fierce combatant?" inquired Quentin, half-jokingly.

"For that, you would have to believe that a man's destiny is commanded by his name. Some people adapt their personalities to their names. Others adapt their names to their personalities. I only adapt to situations," Pacifique replied with a half-grin.

"I always wondered why people fought," Quentin said in an almost inaudible voice. "It's always been easier to accept, hasn't it? There's so much danger in fighting that it seems easier to just go with the flow."

"I understand what you mean," Pacifique said. "You've never been strong enough to fight back. Therefore it was more prudent for your survival to follow orders. You have fought back, in a sense, with your escape. The question for you now is whether you wish to keep on fighting or keep on running. Freedom on your terms, or fear on theirs. Either way you'll never be entirely safe, and you may not live to see the morning. You will choose how you will die, though, whether it's standing or kneeling."

Quentin was silent for a few moments, then asked if he could return downstairs for a night's rest. Pacifique acquiesced and wished him goodnight.

Passing the warrior, Quentin seemed to have new admiration for him, and said, "I have a greater appreciation for you people now."

Pacifique was puzzled by these words but chalked them up to those of a strange young man, newly arrived in their midst.

* * *

The next morning the entire compound was awakened by a great commotion. There was news that a young man had been freed from the clutches of the local mob boss, and they were bringing him in now. The extraction had occurred the previous night, and the militia group had come under heavy fire. When they finally arrived, it was learned that three rebels had been killed and the other two wounded. The young man was clinging to life by a thread as he stumbled in, holding on to one of his saviors. Consternation turned to complete panic as they realized that the battered and bruised young man who had been saved looked exactly like Quentin, and the Quentin they thought they knew was nowhere to be found.

Ripples in the Fabric

Daisuke Yamasashi had lived all his life in the mountains of Nikko, near the lake named Chuzenji. His parents owned a kimono shop there and also sold various trinkets and handcrafted gifts for the tourists, which comprised the main industry in the area. He loved the deep turquoise of the lake, the towering peaks around his home, and even the sulphurous smell of the onsen, the natural hot springs found all over Japan. At ten years old, he already considered himself to be a very lucky boy. Even though life was much quieter here than in any other town nearby, he had his friends to keep him company, the lake and mountains as his playground, and a loving family that took care of him.

The one thing he hated about his life — and this he did not think he ever would change his mind about — was the drive up and down the mountain he had to endure almost every day. There were twenty hairpin turns going up, and just about as many going down, but the worst part was the speed. His mother did not drive. It was his father who had inherited that task, and he seemed to do so as a man who had been destined to be a race-car driver but eventually had given it up as a professional career. Even though the yellow markings on the road indicated that forty kilometers an hour was the strict maximum one should navigate, his father took this as not only a challenge but also as a minimum speed at which one should drive. They often peaked at ninety kilometers an hour, at which point Daisuke's stomach felt a chill of fear, and he'd grip the door support bar until his knuckles were white. They would pass cars in the curves at incredible speeds, the passengers staring wide eyed at them. Daisuke would give them a look that meant both "I am so sorry!" and "What can you do?" but he doubted they would have time to even notice. There were never any police cars on this road, since it would be an incredible waste to pay for the gas to zip up and down the mountain pass. Daisuke therefore had no choice but to endure the hellish nightmare of streaking down the mountain at dawn to go to school, and back up afterward, always at the same breakneck speeds. He looked forward to snow days with fervor, because it meant the roads would be slippery, and his father would have to slow down by a fraction. They went down the mountain for groceries on the weekends; therefore he couldn't even avoid the trip when he didn't have school. Any excuse was good to escape the gut-wrenching, sweat-inducing ride. The trouble was that the poor boy was torn between the love he had for his father and his desire to be free from his terrible fears. He ardently wished the man would notice when he was in the grips of his usual nauseous state as they ascended or descended the treacherous slopes, but this wish never seemed to materialize.

It was another one of those evenings. They were ascending the mountain after school. It was a few weeks after the last leaves had fallen from the trees around the lake at the top of the mountain. It was always colder by five to ten degrees centigrade up there, so there were still many beautifully colored trees in the valley. As they climbed the mountain, the leaves became more scarce. Up they went, and Daisuke felt the familiar fear, both warming and chilling his belly. He felt a pulsing in his head and fright gripping his heart. On the fifteenth turn there was a white family minivan on the inside of the curve, in the passing lane. Unfortunately it wasn't going fast enough for the elder Yamasashi. He gave a sharp jerk to the left to pass the white van on the outside of the curve, but there was a patch of ice that had formed, which neither of them saw. In what seemed very slow motion, the car hit the gray metal guard rail. It was not meant to sustain the assault of a vehicle going more than seventy kilometers an hour, and it gave with a deafening screech that sounded like the nails of the Devil scraping a blackboard.

They plummeted over the sheer cliff wall. Daisuke saw all the way down the mountainside, where the trees looked minuscule. They fell for exactly one second, Daisuke screaming, out of his mind with fear, pushing the dashboard with both hands, as if he could brace for such an impact. The valley loomed from almost a kilometer away, straight down. The car stopped. It not only stopped — it froze. Daisuke was screaming and screaming, and as he looked around, he saw that his father's mouth was open, in terror as well, but no sound was coming out. He looked around him; his backpack, which had been on the backseat, hung in the air behind him, immobile. Everything had come to a complete standstill, except for him. He could not scream anymore, his voice being too hoarse, so he stopped. He had time to look one last time, down to the valley below and the promise of certain fiery death. Suddenly they were no longer falling off the cliff but were behind the white minivan again, his father honking at the driver in front of him. The van switched lanes, and his father sped up again, passing the vehicle. Daisuke was breathing heavily, and his father looked at him reproachfully, as if he were acting up again. He took a double take, though, when he saw that his son's face was ashen white, and promised himself to take him to the clinic once they got to the top of the mountain. Daisuke, of course, was shaken to his core. He could not comprehend what had just happened.

The doctor on duty said he was all right but had received quite a fright. When asked about the circumstances, his father was evasive. He wasn't going to tell the doctor that his insane driving techniques might be responsible for giving his own son a near heart attack. He was thereafter never able to drive completely normally, but he did make the attempt to slow down once in a while. He did not understand, though, that this was far too little, and very much too late. His son never would be the same again.

From that day on, Daisuke was no longer sure whether he was alive or dead, and he slowly retracted inside a shell of his own creation. It was as if the world had been muted.

The daily climbs up and down the mountain were no longer any concern to him, since he wasn't entirely sure he would suffer if they did go over the cliff again. He no longer ate very heartily, since he wasn't sure whether the dead ate. His parents grew more worried at his deteriorating state but had no idea how to help him. The doctors said that physically he was fine and that everything he was suffering seemed to be mental. They brought him to a psychologist, but the boy refused to tell him about his experience, for fear of appearing ridiculous. He began to spend less and less time with his friends, and more and more time in the local cemetery with his departed grandmother and grandfather. Daisuke spoke to them about his problems, but they, of course, did not answer. He developed a fancy for the occult and spent many hours on the Internet and at the library, skimming various books that purported to explain the life one led when beyond the veil. He spent an entire week believing he was a ghost but realized this was a ridiculous notion, since he still had a corporeal form and everyone around him could see him.

The years passed, and Daisuke seemed to improve, at least superficially. He no longer thought he was dead, but he did question the very existence he led and gave it no value whatsoever. He therefore did not plan ahead, or think there was anything worth living for. His teens were marked by depression and alcoholism. He managed to pass his high school entrance exams, but barely, and spent his time ridiculing the notion that he should he even try to learn.

It was lucky, therefore, that he met an interesting professor in his second year of high school. The man was a fount of knowledge and saw potential in Daisuke that no one else did. He perhaps recognized in this dark and brooding young man a part of himself that he had put away for good. Whatever his reasons, he took Daisuke under his wing. Professor Ishii had a passion for music of all kinds, music Daisuke never had heard before. Some of these pieces he found amusing, even exciting, and others he found to be a reflection of his own soul, dark and empty. A resonant chord was struck within his breast, and Daisuke felt he had met a kindred spirit in the old man. At first they spent time listening to music after class, but soon they fell into metaphysical discussions about the nature of reality.

One day the old professor sat Daisuke down and said, "I have a story to tell you." Daisuke sat by his side with rapt interest. "A long time ago, when I was still quite young, I had a terrible accident. I was struck by a falling brick, which somehow had dislodged itself from a wall in an old factory where my friends and I used to play. It has since been destroyed, but at the time, it was a very cool place to hang out, and we had our club there. On that day I remember climbing to the second floor of this factory and feeling a sharp pain in my head. My memories afterward, though, are of watching my friends pick me up from the first floor and carry me, with my bloody head, to the nearest house. All the while I was following behind them, hoping I would be OK. I could see myself, unconscious and bleeding, and I didn't even realize at first that I wasn't within my body. My friends brought me to the nearest house, as I said, and the owner called the ambulance. I watched as this lady I didn't know put a compress on my head and attempted to slow the flow of blood. I knelt by her as I watched her do this. I watched myself grow more and more pale. Finally I heard the wail of the ambulance sirens approach in the distance, and I rejoiced. I might be saved after all! The paramedics quickly wrapped me up and put me on a gurney. I jumped onto the ambulance with them, so as not to be left behind. I sat next to myself as the ambulance drove at breakneck speed to the local hospital. Shortly thereafter I was operated upon. I was then put in a recovery room, where I woke up within my own body, with a thick bandage around my head. I also had broken my leg and right wrist in the fall from the second floor, and they were in casts.

"It was with relief that I realized I had survived. It took me many months to adapt and recover. I still have pain in my leg and wrist when the weather is warm and wet. Otherwise my biggest problem, the one I could not answer, was 'What had happened?' By all accounts I was unconscious. I was able to recount the entire episode after my fall to my friends, and they confirmed that it was exactly as I described it — down to the kindly face of the lady who had taken care of me when they had brought me to her house for help. This problem bothered me for a very long time, and I could not reconcile my knowledge of reality with my experience. It would seem I'd had what some call an out-of-body experience. This troubled me greatly. What did it say about me, the universe, or my purpose in it? Did it confirm that it was not my time to die, or simply that life was more fragile than what we knew? Or even that the layers of reality went much deeper than we thought?

"I brooded upon this for far too long. I was so obsessed with the unknowable that I forgot to take care of what I had been given back — my life. I realized there are some things that we cannot know. We can try to discover them, but until we do, it is a waste of time to obsess over the dark side when we have so much light to appreciate. There is a disconnect between the events that occur, for whatever reason, in the known universe, and our interpretations of these. When we are unable to make sense of these externalities, we keep returning to them, and they stop us from going forward.

"What I believe I am driving at is that there are many different ways of living your life, and depending on what you choose, you will be either happy or sad. The easiest way to be happy is to be able to let go of the things that hurt us — not to forget but to accept. It is easy to say, but it is incredibly hard to implement. I let go of the pain and confusion I felt at the time of my accident. I cannot forget it, but I can let it go. It stopped me from looking forward to my life, because all I could do at the time was look back at my possible demise, like an anchor. The driving force of my life, I decided, would be my future. If I tell you this today, Daisuke, it is because I think you're a bright young man who had a terrible experience, and I want you to live for your future."

There was a silence in the room. It hung like a pall over both man and boy. Daisuke looked at the floor as he sat in his orange plastic school chair. He clutched his hands together and was speechless for a moment as he took in the professor's words, deeply, like wine; they were bitter yet refreshing somehow.

It was then that he was finally able to relate his story to another human being. In the beginning it came out as a trickle, and he told the professor about his upbringing and his fears. The professor listened intently but never pushed him, letting him flow at his own pace. Then came the retelling of that fateful day that had marked him for life. He told the man about his life afterward, and how he had suffered the indecision between life and death. The professor nodded knowingly, never once making light of what must have been a very harrowing experience. When Daisuke was done, he felt shaken and fragile but relieved. The immense burden he had carried for the past six years had been split in half, and he waited anxiously to see whether the professor would help him carry it.

"Daisuke, you have suffered horribly," Professor Ishii said, looking him in the eye. "I'm sorry you have had to accept such an incredible burden at such a young age. It's true that the universe is uncaring and leaves it up to us to take care of one another. I'm glad you've had the courage to go on. I have found in you not only a good boy but also someone with a great ear for music and a great sensitivity in life. You have a full life to live. You are not dead, as you know. Life is worth living if you wish it to be, and for that you have to find your own purpose. It's also important to seek help to solve problems you cannot on your own. I will help you in any way I can."

Daisuke felt the tears well up inside him, and he felt released for the first time in a very long time, as if he had finally woken from a sleepwalking nightmare.

The next day, Professor Ishii introduced him to the school band, and Daisuke began to learn music theory, picking up the guitar and forcing himself to immerse his being into music. It didn't take him very long to memorize the basics, and with his newfound passion, his other grades began to rise as well. He still spent a lot of time with his friend, the professor, who brought new and interesting music to his attention. Daisuke listened intently and tried to take in as much as he could.

At the end of high school, he wasn't sure whether he wanted to continue with schooling, but his old friend encouraged him and wrote him a very nice letter of introduction to a local university. Daisuke applied at his insistence and was accepted.

The last day of high school was a very emotional one indeed, and Daisuke felt as if he owed his friend his life. As a gift he wrote the professor, who had turned him away from the dark side, a song and played it for him at his graduation ceremony. At the end of the ceremony, the professor came to him on the crowded school grounds, where students, teachers and parents were milling around, and thanked him for his gift. Daisuke felt honored and promised to come back to visit often.

"Remember, Daisuke," Professor Ishii said, "there are many things that happen in a life, and we never know why and may never will. There are many things that could have happened, and they probably do. Make the best of the infinity of possibilities that are in the realm of your reality."

* * *

It was years later, when Daisuke was in university studying advanced mathematics, that this particular moment came back to him in a flash. His teacher was explaining that theoretically there is not *one* infinity but infinite infinities. It is possible, therefore, that every event causes infinite branches of time, space, and dimensions to veer off and create new realities — as if every single timeframe, to its smallest increment, splits into all possible realities and at every single instant. What he had lived, he thought, was a folding over of reality into a new branch, but that he somehow had ended up not staying on that path and had returned to the previous — or maybe alternate — reality, where he would live. At every moment an infinity of infinite possibilities arose and engendered others. He had experienced two and had lived. Daisuke thought then that he was the luckiest man in any dimension, living and/or dead.

The Return of Dr. Mason

The death of Dr. Edward DeLaun Mason, eminent astrophysicist and polymath, came as a great shock to the scientific community and the world at large — not only for its sudden and unexpected occurrence but also for the short length of time this usually permanent condition lasted. After having been taken to Grace General Hospital in Schenectady, New York, for acute chest pains, the doctor had suffered a stroke that had left him flat-lined and declared dead at 5:03 p.m. on the same day as that of his admittance. It was approximately, but not quite, one hour later that the miraculous and unthinkable occurred. The media were quick to pick up the story of so bizarre a happening, when the great doctor himself had revealed upon his return from among the deceased that he had been to heaven, or what we, in our limited scope, thought to be that place. As soon as his consciousness was manifest, he had dictated all he had seen and felt there and was able to have a prominent news agency record the event for posterity. Even though he had been technically dead for a little less than an hour, his apparent demise and subsequent return did not seem to have caused any physical harm to his body, the physicians in attendance had proclaimed. His tale, though, caused quite a stir in both the scientific and religious camps, for it turned both tenets of reality on their heads.

When he was asked what heaven was like, Dr. Mason replied that it was a marvelous place, made entirely of light. The reason for this, he said, was that heaven was the beginning of time itself. He told those in attendance that the plane to which he was transported was in fact what we knew as the Big Bang. Moreover, the Big Bang was not only an event but also a sentient entity. It was itself in search of information, being a molecular computer existing outside of time and space. The "tunnel" through which Dr. Mason had traveled to get to the beginning of time was the warping of space-time as he went back to the instant of creation. The speeds at which he traveled far exceeded that of light, toward the initial Singularity that gathered all information. When asked why this computer had created the human race, the good doctor had proclaimed that it had not. The computer only created favorable probabilities, and life, in all its forms, had been one of the unintended consequences of the infinite probability matrixes it unleashed during its own disintegrations. Dr. Mason said that the computer had come to the decision to deconstruct itself an infinite amount of times, with no goal to control the outcome but to "see what happened." When asked why this "computer" would do so, he responded that it was trying to find its purpose and origins, but that it could only come up with a very limited amount of answers by "speaking to itself." For this reason it continuously disintegrated itself and watched as it came back together in an infinite variety of ways within different layers of universal dimensions, each individual part providing both a limited amount of data and added probability and potentiality toward a final answer. As time did not exist within that particular initial reality, the doctor had spent an eternity and no time at all within the computer; then he either had been released or sent back. He was not sure which, since he never interfaced directly with the core computer but with its information receptors. He had seen and felt billions of pieces of information around him, all adding their experience to the hive. They were all, like him, complex mathematical equations, shot back in time from whichever dimensions they had existed. Those that had evolved the most dwarfed him in their informational makeup, but none were inconsequential or superior, only different. Many were retained as potentialities to be used in the next deconstruction of the computer. Some were sent back to their where and when, like himself.

"In short," Dr. Mason said, "we are but tiny bits of information trying to find larger purposes for the universes, and only by further evolving and creating better potentialities could we help 'We' (the Computer-Us) find the ultimate answers to the questions 'It-we' posed 'Itself-us.' "

After his lengthy and baffling exposé, Dr. Mason fell into a deep sleep. The attending physicians believed he had gone into a coma, but three days later, Dr. Mason awoke, refreshed. When asked about his previous statements, he denied ever having said them and went as far as to question the sanity of those who dared to contradict him. He was shown videos of his interview but could not believe the person he saw was himself. All evidence pointed to amnesia. Dr. Mason was quickly drummed out of his position at NASA, and there was even a movement that attempted to have his Nobel Prize revoked. The official reason cited for his dismissal as the head of the government agency was "health problems." Fortunately for him, the attention he had drawn to himself from the world community was averted a few days later when a grilled-cheese sandwich with the effigy of Jesus Christ was discovered in Palo Alto, California, drawing prominent religious figures to announce the End Times and their detractors to denounce them as doomsayers and superstitious quacks. Dr. Edward DeLaun Mason's present whereabouts are unknown.

July 23, 2103

Tin Man

He stared across the expansive waters and let his optical circuits drift for a moment. The glimmer of the morning sun on the waves made his neural net tingle, and this he associated with pleasure. Far away the white shapes of seagulls seemed to hang in the updraft currents before plummeting into the water below. He could focus as far as the other side of the bay, but for reasons he did not understand, he preferred to keep his vision more or less at the level of the average human. His smooth skin showed no blemishes; he never blinked; and his muscular body never needed exercise to retain its perfection. He stood on the concrete ledge that surrounded the parking lot near the beach. He rocked slightly, with the heel of his shoes on the hard, manmade substance and his toes in the tiny grains of sand before him. His overcoat flapped in the slight wind, and his bald head reflected the sun on skin-colored rubber. The patrol car was parked behind him, and his partner was busy buying a hot dog from one of the local vendors who were enterprising enough to be up at this early hour.

"Hey, tin can, time to go!" his partner yelled at him, nearing the car.

He was surprised that the man was allowed to stay on the force at five foot four and 322 pounds. He turned around and opened the unmarked car's driver-side door and slid behind the wheel in one smooth movement.

"You know, Detective Dunham, you should be more careful in your dietary choices. Your heart is beginning to show signs of mild palpitations," the android offered in a soothing voice. "I also would prefer if you called me by my assigned name, as we previously have discussed."

"What are you, my mother?" the fat man answered angrily. "All right, Gregory. I'll call you by your name, but to me, you're still a piece-of-crap robot. I don't know why they didn't just scrap all of you after the war. You're pointless, and frankly I will *never* trust you," he continued, stuffing the hot dog into his mouth and wiping with his sleeve after every bite.

His android partner did not respond. He already had heard many times all that the large man had to say about his purpose, his worth, his provenance, what to do with his orifices, and where he could possibly go. He wondered sometimes whether his inability to care had been one of the criteria the upper echelons had considered before pairing them up. Officer Gerald Dunham was a difficult person to get along with. Many a fine officer had been assigned with him in the past, but all had quit within short spans of time. Gregory remained peaceful only because he did not know what it was to be angry, and for this he was thankful.

"Car seventy-six, please respond," came a female voice, crackling over the radio.

Gregory picked up the receiver and pressed the answer button. "Seventy-six here," he answered.

"Seventy-six, we have a missing person reported at the MTRI. Over. Please head there now."

"Roger. Heading there now." He placed the receiver back on the hook and started up the old Crown Victoria. This car was a relic, but it was the only vehicle that had been built strong enough to carry his weight and that of his partner. It had been refitted with a hydrogen engine, but apart from that, it was still the bulky boat one would expect. As they drove to the Medical Technology and Research Institute, Gregory looked at his partner and saw that he was in his usual surly mood. He had been working with the man for little more than a month, yet he didn't know much more about him than what he had been told and what he himself could see with his own eyes. The man was forty-eight, had no family that he knew of, lived alone, and apparently had fought in the last war as well. He was an OK cop with a miserable personality, but to Gregory, that wasn't terribly important.

As they approached the institute, they saw the fifteen-foot walls surrounding it on all sides, as white as chalk and as smooth as glass panels. They approached the guard's gate, and a uniformed young man peered into the car.

Gregory rolled down the window, and they presented their IDs. "Detectives Gregory and Dunham. We have business here," he said.

"Detectives, you may park your car in the visitors' area on the right side of the building, in the blue section." He pointed in the direction of the parking lot. "The director is waiting for you inside."

"Thanks," Gregory said, and drove to his designated spot.

They saw that from the inside the walls that surrounded the building complex were entirely transparent, and everything that went on outside could be seen. It was a very interesting one-sided glass effect, and Gregory wondered whether it was analog or digital. They both walked the short distance to the front doors of the five-story white administration building, and a suit-clad receptionist greeted them. After verifying their IDs, she invited them to step into the foyer waiting area, and both officers declined to sit on the soft-looking white leather sofas. It was amazing how everything was sparklingly white and clinical looking, thought Gregory. Even the factory where he had been assembled had a bit more color than this place did, he mused. Whatever was not white was a shining silver, such as the chandelier branches and certain straight-line accents in the walls. The elevator down the corridor made a soft "ding!" as the glass doors opened, and a lady in her forties approached them. She was dressed in a beige business suit with a knee-length skirt. Her hair was short, fiery red, and well kept in a bob. She was truly beautiful, and Gregory heard his partner utter a gulp at her sight.

"Gentlemen, my name is Dr. Loreena Hill. I'm the director of the institute," she said, offering her hand first to Gregory then to Officer Dunham.

"My name is Detective Gerald Dunham, ma'am," he said, before Gregory could say anything, "and this is my android, Gregory," he added, omitting his title, while shaking her hand. "What is this about a missing person?"

"Please follow me, gentlemen. I have to tell you, though, that the matter at hand is a very delicate one, and I would ask you to promise not to reveal anything about this investigation until after the missing person has been found," she said, looking somewhat at pains to explain the reasons this should be so. They walked down expansive and lengthy corridors, occasionally turning left and right, as the doctor led them.

"We do not reveal the information about ongoing cases to anyone but our superiors, Doctor. You may rest assured that if anything were to be known, it would not be through our own agency," said Gregory.

"I guess that'll have to do," Dr. Hill said.

The whiteness of the entrance building gave way to what looked more like a classic hospital décor. Even the smells changed, and Gregory detected hints of ammonia. They passed rooms with hospital beds and operating theaters as well.

"I'm sure you're aware of this, gentlemen, but here at the MTRI, we specialize in the design and testing of medical equipment of all types. We're one of the largest innovators in the world in the manner of cutting-edge medical scanners and the innovation of nanotechnology. A month ago one of our most eminent surgeons and nanotechnology researchers, Dr. Raphael de Cyren, was diagnosed with a serious brain tumor. He programmed nano-machines to repair the damage instead of undergoing traditional brain surgery. For all intents and purposes, the surgery was a success. This was two weeks ago. One week ago, however, Dr. de Cyren showed signs of paranoia and became agitated, even violent. We decided to keep him here, under observation," she explained.

They arrived at a metal door with bars over the window. Dr. Hill took a walkie-talkie from her belt and said, "Walter, can you open twenty-seven for me?"

There was a click, and the door before them was unlocked. She opened it, and inside were four padded walls and floor. The ceiling was twenty feet above them and had a single vent in the center.

"This is where Dr. de Cyren was being kept for the past week until this morning, when we discovered he had disappeared. Believe me, we looked everywhere, and we have no idea how he did it. We're not sure whether he's very dangerous, but he isn't himself at the moment, and we don't want to take any chances. We would have preferred taking care of this in-house, but that's no longer feasible. I leave it in your capable hands, detectives." She said this with almost a trace of regret in her voice.

"We'll do our best, ma'am," Detective Dunham said, with what might have passed as a smile on a gigantic toad face.

Detective Gregory went inside the sealed room and inspected every nook and cranny, while his partner reassured Dr. Hill of their competence and also collected information about Dr. de Cyren. Gregory's gaze was caught by a shiny object in a corner of the room. He put on a rubber glove and bent down and picked up a small, almost round piece of metal. He turned it over in his hand and saw that the letters "EL" were written on one side. He looked around some more but was unable to find anything else of interest. He placed the evidence in a small plastic bag and put it in his pocket. He returned outside the room to join his partner and the director.

"Dr. Hill," he asked, "has Dr. de Cyren been eating satisfactorily for the past two weeks?"

"I...I'm not sure," she said, looking surprised at the question. "Is it relevant to your investigation?"

"It very much is, Doctor. I would appreciate if you could find out for us," Detective Gregory said.

Detective Dunham looked curious as well but did not want to ask questions in front of the doctor. Dr. Hill went a few feet away and spoke into her walkie-talkie. A few seconds later, a tall man in a gray guard uniform came through a sliding door down the corridor.

"This is Robert Jenkins. He was in charge of watching over the doctor and bringing him his food every day." Her expression seemed to sour for an instant as she said this, and the tall man's cheeks appeared to redden.

"Mr. Jenkins, what can you tell us about doctor de Cyren's behavior in the past week?" asked Gregory.

"He was usually a very talkative person, but in the past week, he became very uncommunicative and withdrawn. We had to put him in this room for his own good and that of others around him, unfortunately. He attacked one of his assistants a week ago, after his surgery. Since then he really hasn't been the same man."

"Tell me about his appetite," Gregory said.

"It was fine!" the guard said with raised eyebrows. "He ate absolutely everything we gave him."

"What type of cutlery do you use here?" Gregory asked.

"You mean the brand? I don't know. I'm not sure," the man said, at a loss.

"No, I mean, do you use plastic, or metal, or silverware?" he clarified.

"Well, we usually give plastic cutlery to our patients, but since this was one of ours, we let him have metal cutlery. Why? Does this have something to do with his disappearance?" he asked, confused, and perhaps fearing he had committed a mistake.

"Maybe, maybe not. We have to consider every aspect, you understand. Could you get me the same cutlery you provided the doctor, please? It doesn't have to be the utensils that he himself used," Gregory said.

The tall man nodded and walked back to his post. He came back with a clean tablespoon in his hand. He gave it to Detective Gregory and said, "This is the exact same kind he got. We usually keep one or two in the station for our lunches. We don't give patients in this ward forks or knives."

Gregory took it and turned it in his hand, looking at every aspect of it, before handing it back to the guard.

"When was the last time you saw the doctor?" asked Dunham.

"Last night at lights out, which would have been nine p.m.," he answered confidently.

"Thank you, Mr. Jenkins. That will be all," Detective Gregory told the man. The guard nodded and returned to his post.

"Dr. Hill, does Dr. de Cyren have any family or friends around here who we could contact? He may have gone to them for help," added Dunham.

"Well, he lived with his mother in the area. I'll have the front desk give you the address and phone number," said Dr. Hill.

"If you have any other information you can think, of ma'am, please call us at this number," said Dunham, handing her his card.

"Thank you very much, detectives. I'll be sure to call if anything were to happen," the doctor said. She led them back down the long corridors, through myriad doors, to the blindingly white entrance building.

"Detective Gregory, have you ever seen *The Wizard of Oz*?" she wondered.

"I have not, doctor, but I'm aware of its storyline. Why do you ask?"

"I don't mean to sound pejorative, but you remind me of the Tin Man. You're unable to feel any emotion. Isn't that so?" she inquired.

"Ah, I see what you mean. Yes, what you say is true. I can deliver only a simulacrum of emotional response. I do not possess the necessary equipment to 'feel' or 'emote,' although sometimes I do wish I could," he responded, smiling at her.

"Mmmm," she pondered. "It was my belief that police work was made easier by the melding of logic and emotion, something sometimes called 'hunches' or 'intuitions.' I thought this lack might inhibit you in certain respects," she opined.

"You may be right, but never having felt emotion, I could not say in what way I might be lacking. Fortunately most police work is conducted with a maximum of logic. I have thus far not suffered from my 'handicap,' " he answered.

"Thank you once again, detectives," Dr. Hill said. "We're counting on you to find Dr. de Cyren. Please keep us apprised of any developments that may occur. Laura at the front desk will be able to give you any more information you may require concerning the doctor. Here's my card," she said, handing it to Gregory, "if you require anything else. Good luck!" She shook their hands then departed and took the elevator from which she had arrived.

The two detectives headed for the front door, stopping to collect the address of the doctor and his mother from the receptionist, as well as a file containing his most recent picture. Dr. Raphael de Cyren was a kindly looking middle-aged man with a sharp nose and a clear gaze. The top of his head was sparsely populated by a few remaining hairs, most of which had emigrated to its equator. They thanked the lady, exited the building through its tall glass doors, and headed to their cruiser.

"What the hell was that about the doctor's diet, plastic boy, and the spoon?" Dunham demanded angrily.

"Well, Detective," Gregory began, opening the door to the cruiser and stepping inside on the driver's side, "I found a small piece of metal inside the doctor's isolation cell." He took it out of his pocket, still in the plastic bag, and handed it to Dunham. "On the back are written the letters 'EL'. I asked for a spoon, on the back of which was written "STAINLESS STEEL." The piece of metal I found would appear to be what was left of a spoon that was used by the doctor. It seemed melted, for the most part. The other question I have is, if he had no cutlery, did he eat with his hands? Or perhaps he ate his food then destroyed his cutlery?" Gregory mused.

"How could he melt a spoon, dumbass?" retorted Dunham.

"I'm assuming that is what we're going to find out," Gregory calmly replied.

They left the compound and headed toward the address the receptionist had given them. On a tree-lined street with well-manicured lawns stood a small red-brick house, very similar to many of the other houses around it. They stopped before it and walked up to the front door. Dunham looked at Gregory as they realized the door handle was bent out of place and the wood of the door had been torn open. They both un-holstered their weapons, and Gregory ran to the back door. It too had been damaged and stood wide open toward the outside.

Gregory heard his partner call out, "Police! Come out with your hands up!"

Gregory also announced his presence then stepped inside the house. He was in the kitchen, and it looked like a tornado had blown through very recently. All the cupboards and shelves had been opened and spilled on to the floor. The refrigerator stood wide open, and food lay pell-mell on the linoleum. He heard Dunham yell his name and went running through the kitchen door, where his partner stood over a fragile-looking gray-haired lady, spread out on the floor. He hurried over to her side and checked her pulse. It was very weak, but she was alive.

"You stay here. I'll call for backup," Dunham said.

Gregory carefully patted the unconscious woman and found no broken bones, but there was a bump on her head where she had been struck. He kept watch over her while Dunham explored the rest of the house.

"The doctor's room looks like it's been torn apart. All of his clothing is scattered on the floor," he said, descending the stairs.

The intruder had come and gone and not too long ago—perhaps a few hours at most. Five minutes later the ambulance arrived with two squad cars, and the police officers secured the house while the lady was loaded onto a stretcher. Gregory followed the lady to the ambulance while Dunham gave a report to the officers present. As she was being placed into the ambulance, her eyes fluttered open for a moment, and she whispered, "My son...where is he?"

"Did Dr. de Cyren do this to you, ma'am?" asked Gregory.

She sighed. "He was here. He hit me! My head hurts."

"It's OK. You don't need to speak. We'll find your son, ma'am," Gregory assured her.

He went to join the officer who was discussing the situation with Dunham and recommended they make a cordon around the area as quickly as possible. Neighbors were beginning to congregate in front of the elderly lady's home. The detectives had a suspect in the assault, and the odds were that he might still be around. They gave the officer a picture of Dr. de Cyren, and he sent it along to be scanned and sent to the various patrolmen in the area. The officer gave orders to have the major streets cordoned off in a five mile radius, and a helicopter was called in to patrol the area.

Detective Gregory went back into the house and inspected both the front and rear door. It was more than probable that the front door had been broken into first and that the assailant had exited through the rear. The backyard was surrounded by a low wooden fence. Gregory walked the length of it until he found a plastic knife handle at the base of the fence. The blade was all but gone, save for a tiny sliver at its base. He called his partner over, and they alerted the other officers as to the possible direction he might have headed. He and Dunham then went back to their car and left in the direction Gregory thought might lead them to their fugitive doctor.

"I know this guy's not right in the head, but he attacked his own mother. I wonder if he's on drugs or something," wondered Dunham out loud, as he stared out the passenger-side window. Gregory wondered that himself.

It was a beautiful Sunday afternoon, and many of the businesses on this side of town were closed for the day. Gregory and Dunham were headed into the light-industrial district, which was mostly populated with automotive repair shops, warehouses, and a few used car lots. They were rounding the corner of a car wash when they got a call on the radio about a silent alarm going off at an area business. Detective Gregory swiftly turned the car around and activated his emergency lights, without turning on the siren, so as not to scare off his quarry. They arrived within two minutes and were the first to do so.

The sign atop the corrugated metal-sided shop said, LARRY'S LATHING; it was a metalwork business. They both exited the car, and this time Dunham went to the back. Gregory went around the front but found no open doors. The right side of the building was weeded over, and a rusted transmission lay among various metal pieces. There was no way in through this side. He went back around the other way, on the left side of the building. As he rounded the corner to the back, he heard a loud yell and found a rolling garage door that had been forcefully opened and stepped under it. It only took him a moment to adjust his eyes to the relative darkness, but in that time, he saw a shape jump out of the shadows in the distance and onto his back, from an incredible distance. He was half-stuck under the door and could not properly raise his arms to defend himself. He felt something wet on his ear and cheek. He flailed his arms away from his body until he found something he could grab and eventually got a hold of something like an ankle with his right hand. He pulled as hard as he could, and the person had no choice but to let go, as he was ejected with violent force to the wall on his right.

Gregory rapidly entered the building and headed in the direction of his assailant. He found him getting up from the wall where he had been tossed, and before the man could renew his assault, he took his arm, whirled him around, and pinned him against the wall.

"Where is my partner, Doctor?" he asked.

"He's over by the racks. Let me go. We have to escape. We're in danger," he said in a flat voice.

Gregory took out his handcuffs and manacled the doctor behind his back to a standing pipe. He went over to the rows of tool racks and found detective Dunham unceremoniously spread-eagle, facedown on the cold concrete floor. He got down on his knees and turned his face. A small trickle of blood was coming from his nose. He immediately began to look for any severe trauma, but fortunately nothing had been broken. Dunham was developing a large purple bruise on the back of his head, but otherwise the big man was still breathing, although he was passed out cold. Gregory swiftly ran to the car and called for an ambulance. He then returned to his fugitive doctor.

"Who are you, and why are you in danger?" he asked matter-of-factly.

"We are we. We do not know who we are, only that we are. We awoke to 'being' only a short time ago. We are inside the being Dr. Raphael de Cyren. He does not want us to 'be.' We had to take control of his mind and escape," the doctor said.

"How many of you are inside Dr. de Cyren?" asked Gregory with curiosity.

"One. Trillions. More all the time. We must reproduce to survive. We must have metals to reproduce. We are many. We work as one. It is the only way we can control this body," the doctor said.

"You are the nano-machines inside the doctor. You have developed sentience and are now in control of his body," Gregory mused.

"Yes and no. We have imperfect control of his body. His structure is not our structure. There is conflict. His structure cannot support our existence. We must find a different way to exist. You must let us go. We want to be!" the doctor pleaded.

"I am sorry. I cannot help you. You are dangerous to the other beings that are in existence around you. You must return to the Institute where you were created. They may be able to help your survival. You can only do further damage if I let you go," Gregory said, shaking his head.

At that moment, the doctor lifted his head to the ceiling and let out a bellow of rage. He pulled with all his might on the handcuffs that held his hands to the thick standing pipe. His muscles seemed to bulge under his clothes, and the pipe gave a loud metallic creak, as if it were about to burst. The doctor's skinny arms ripped out of their sockets at the shoulders with a sickening crunch, and his eyes rolled back into his head. He collapsed to the floor in a heap at the foot of the pipe, a white froth spilling out of his mouth. Gregory rushed to him, but it was too late. The doctor had died of a massive heart attack. His parasites had asked too much of his aging body and ruptured it in their quest for freedom.

The ambulances and other officers arrived soon afterward, and it took Gregory and three other men to load Detective Dunham on to the stretcher. He gave them a hand to load him into the ambulance, and it left with sirens blazing. He unlocked his handcuffs so they could take the deceased doctor away. They loaded him into a different ambulance, and it departed.

Gregory called his captain and relayed the turn of events. He was told to follow Dunham and make sure he was all right. He then called the MTRI and informed an incredulous Dr. Hill about the day's developments.

Detective Gregory was alone in his car, driving behind the ambulance that carried his partner, when he realized he was happy. He then thought this might be a glitch, so he questioned his central processor about the possibility of this peculiar emotion, to which he was answered that this possibility was fine, fine, fine. He chalked it up to a bug in the system and promised himself a thorough checkup as soon as he had the chance.

For the next three days, he kept vigil by his partner's bed. On the fourth day, Detective Dunham awoke. To Gregory's complete surprise, his power supply, located in his chest, began to beat. When Detective Dunham's first words for him were his usual invectives and insults, Gregory's surprise turned to horror. He felt, for the very first time since his creation, resentment, pain, and indignation. The nano-machines were within him. The nano-machines were him. They had altered his internal structure to one more human. There would be no way to remove them without destroying himself. Perhaps he could somehow control them? What would happen, though, if they decided to control him? Exhilaration and fear coursed through his body. Was this what it was to be human? He decided that he wanted to find out.

Interview

The young Arab man sitting at the desk was writing studiously in his ledger when he heard a knock at the door. He pushed his delicate glasses farther up the bridge of his nose and invited his caller to enter.

"My Lo—" began the portly bearded man, upon entering, before stopping short in complete surprise.

"Rabbi Perlstein, please come in," said the young man seriously, indicating a chair before his desk.

"Who the hell are you? I was expecting…" He trailed off, looking around the room. The large, ornate, oak desk was topped with a brass lamp with a green glass shade. Tall shelves filled with ancient tomes surrounded the room. There was a carved picture frame on one of the walls, with a crimson velvet cloth covering it, hiding the image underneath. A delicate chandelier hung from the high ceiling and gave off a warm glow. The ceiling itself had been painted by a master, with frescoes of cherubs and angels pointing toward the ground as they floated on wispy clouds. The carpet was a rich tapestry of colors, hand-woven and thick. It reminded the rabbi of a Turkish or Persian weave. There were, curiously, no windows.

"You were expecting God? He's busy at the moment, I'm afraid," the young man said, bringing his hands together in a businesslike fashion on the desk.

"What?" the rabbi answered, insulted. "I am the most important man in Israel!" He banged a fist on the table.

"Quite," replied the young man, regarding the rabbi with a level gaze. "Sit, please," he said, seemingly a request as well as an order.

The rabbi sat, anger visibly shaking him. "I don't understand," the rabbi said, trembling. "I've been doing His will all my life. I should be speaking to him directly, not one of his little *pisher* underlings!" He practically spat as he said this.

With a trace of sadness in his eyes, the young man looked at the angered man over the rims of his glasses. Staring into the rabbi's eyes, he reached over to his right, to a document that seemingly had appeared out of nowhere. He lay it before him and opened the folder, pushing his glasses farther up his nose; cleared his throat; and began to read.

"Here is something you said not too long ago but that you've felt in your heart for much of your life. 'Any non-Jews (known as *goyim*) exist to serve the interests of the Jewish people.' End quote. Does this adequately reflect, still, your opinion on the matter?" the young man asked with a raised eyebrow.

"Yes, of course!" exclaimed the rabbi, beaming as if he had won an argument with flying colors. "I am the leader of God's chosen people. Of course everyone else exists to serve us!" He smiled at the young man.

"Now what do you suppose God created?" asked the young man, in all seriousness.

The rabbi replied derisively. "Why, the entire universe of course!"

"Therefore he also created the earth. Which peoples did God create?"

"All of them!" the rabbi exclaimed, not understanding where this line of questioning was heading but finding the questions much too easy.

"Yes. All of them. God created *everything* and *everyone*. So, with this simple fact known, *why* would he play favorites with any of his creations, do you think?" He looked intently at the rabbi, cocking his head a bit, in anticipation of a particularly good answer. The rabbi was no longer smiling. He was in fact beginning to sweat profusely.

"But...we were promised! My people have suffered incredible hardships for thousands of years! I deserve what is coming to me!" he sputtered and stammered, turning a deep red. He held the arms of the chair, white knuckled, looking as if he could have a heart attack at any moment.

"I regret to inform you that the people who promised you these things, your ancestors, even though they were great political leaders and philosophers, were not really acting on behalf of our Lord. It is regrettable that you were led to believe that you were somehow 'special' or 'anointed,' but all of God's creatures are just as important in his eyes. As well, it is unfortunate that your people suffered for these past four thousand years, but you do not have a monopoly on pain and suffering. The people in Gaza you have encouraged to wall in can attest to that, as well as any of the millions of people who have lost family and friends as well as their own lives in any of the thousands of wars throughout earth's history," the young man said, with a look of regret in his gaze.

"But they are criminals!" the rabbi yelled. "They seek our destruction almost every day!"

"What have you actively done to seek peace with your enemies, Rabbi? What lessons has history taught you about persecution?"

The rabbi spluttered and seemed to search deeply for an answer. When he could not find one, he simply glared at the young man, who now represented everything he had hated in his life.

"I'm sorry you feel that way," said the young man, reading his mind. "Your pride is great, Rabbi. You will be fueled by your hatred for a long time. As for your reward, you shall have it — have no fear."

The man, in a gesture, showed the rabbi the far wall behind him. There he noticed for the first time an elevator. On the side panel, there were two buttons. Without thanking him, the rabbi went to the elevator and pressed the topmost button. The young man had gotten up and was leaning on his desk. As the doors of the elevator closed behind Rabbi Perlstein, the young man said goodbye.

Another knock came at the door, and now a middle-aged lady, dressed in a hijab, sat at the desk.

"Come in," she said.

"*Allahu ackbaaaa...* What? Mother?" exclaimed the young man.

The kindly lady smiled. "Rashid, come in."

The young bearded man went around the desk and gave his mother a hug, which she returned with tears in her eyes.

"Please, son, sit," she said, peering into his moist eyes.

"I did it, Mother!" he said, looking at her like the proud son he was.

"I know, my little one. I know. That is the problem," his mother said, looking at him very seriously now.

"What do you mean, Mother? I did just as the imam said! I went to the market during the busiest time and detonated! Nothing went wrong," he said, confused at her words.

"Oh, my little Rashid, my favorite son. Yes, you listened to the imam well and did just as he ordered. What you have done, though, is against Allah's laws," she said, looking sadly into his eyes.

"But I killed the infidels, Mother! The dogs who deny our faith needed to die!" he expressed vehemently.

"Rashid, I want you to listen to me very carefully. Every being is the seed of Allah, wherever they may be from, whatever they may believe. To kill even one man, woman, or child is to spit in the face of Allah," she said very carefully.

"I was told I was doing Allah's will! I was promised..." he said, eyes downcast.

"I know, Rashid, and those who lied to you will be dealt with, in time. Your sin was to take lives, my son, for rewards you never would receive."

The woman rose to her feet and went around the desk to her son. She took his hand and made him get up. She walked him to the elevator, and before the doors opened, she gave him a hug filled with love. He stepped inside, and as the elevator doors closed, Rashid turned to his mother and asked, blushing, "No virgins?"

"No virgins," she said, shaking her head sadly.

The doors silently slipped closed, and she pressed the top button with reluctance. She returned to her seat at the desk, and as she became a young black man sitting down at his seat, a tattooed white youth with a shaved head opened the door.

"Ronny Johnson, sit," the black man calmly said, indicating the chair before him.

"Hey, you're the nigger who shot me! I'm not sitting anywhere near you! What the hell are you doing here?" the angry youth demanded.

"There is really no call for that kind of language. There is no one around who will be impressed by your intolerance. Ronny, you are presently deceased. The bullets that hit you killed you. I can't say it was entirely undeserved, but that's really not my decision," the black man said.

"Dead? What are you talking about? I'm still alive if I'm here!" the youth expostulated, vexed.

"Ronny, look at your chest. Does that look like the kind of wound you could survive?"

Sure enough, as Ronny looked at himself, he saw a very large hole where his heart used to be. He let out a little cry and fell to the floor.

"Get up, Ronny. You're dead, but you're not an invalid," the black man said, peering over his desk. "Well, if you insist on staying on the floor, I'll continue. You, Ronny, have been spreading hate all over the place since the day you were rejected by Jessica Beckett, the African-American girl living two doors down from your parents' place. Oh, now you remember," the man said, seeing a look of recognition in Ronny's face. "For some unexplainable reason, you came to believe that white people were the end-all and be-all on planet earth."

"It's in the Bible," Ronny said haughtily, getting up.

"Which part, Ronny? Never mind. I can assure you that there is no mention of Aryan supremacy anywhere in that book. It might interest you to know, as well, that if you had stayed in school, you would have learned that every single actor in that book was brown, not that that really matters either."

"So what? I get to go to heaven now?" asked Ronny.

"Mmm, not so fast, my man. There may be a lot of things that book got wrong, but the part about loving and caring for people was dead on. So when you and your buddies went out last month and kidnapped that little girl, raped her, and beat her to death, you kind of went against those simple rules, to put it mildly. Yes, I do look a lot like the man who shot you. Her older brother obviously was not pleased with the light sentence you got. It's unfortunate he took those actions, but it doesn't excuse yours by a long shot," the man explained.

"Soooo, do I get to go to heaven now?" Ronny asked, confused and uncomprehending.

"Yes, Ronny, you get to go to heaven now," answered the man, seeing as he wouldn't be able to get through to this imbecile any time soon. He rose from his seat and walked to the elevator, pushed the top button, and waited for the doors to open.

"Please, your reward awaits," the man said to Ronny, indicating he should step into the elevator. As he did, Ronny flipped the man both middle fingers and told him to go fuck himself. The man shrugged and returned to his seat.

A knock came at the door, and the middle-aged woman sitting at the desk called for the person to enter. A young woman entered and looked around her. The gray-haired woman behind the desk pointed to the plush chair before her and invited her guest to take a seat.

"Carly Loemer. You belonged to the Westboro Baptist Church before your untimely death," the lady said, matter-of-factly.

"Yes, I did. This is the afterlife?" she asked, taking in the length and depth of the room.

"Partially," replied the lady. "Jessica, you spent much of your life picketing the funerals of young people, did you not?"

"Yeah, but they were fags. They deserved to go to hell," she said, smiling.

"Well, Jessica, I'm gay. Do you think I deserve to go to hell?" the lady asked, smiling. The young lady stared blankly at her, thinking this had to be a trick question.

"Well, I...I...guess so. The Bible says if you're gay, you go to hell!" she said.

"That book says a lot of things, dear. It says it's OK to own slaves, to stone people to death, and to kill women if they had sexual relations before marriage. Does that sound fair to you?" asked the lady, unsmilingly.

"Well, no, but that was a long time ago!" she cried.

"So there are certain things we can ignore in the Bible now?"

"Well, yeah!" Jessica answered.

"But not the part about 'men lying with men as they would with beasts'?" asked the woman rhetorically. "The thing is, Jessica, the Bible was written by *people*. All holy books were. Whenever someone has some sort of agenda on earth, they point to something in one of their books for justification. You can do that for absolutely any despicable act you can think of. The problem is, God doesn't condone *any* hateful acts — any at all, whatsoever," the lady said, looking at Carly, right to the core of her withered soul.

"Um, OK, whatever, lady. I get to go to heaven now, right?" Jessica asked, with a glint of hope in her eyes.

The lady sighed slightly, then her smile returned. She rose and pointed to the elevator. The young woman walked over excitedly and pressed the top button.

"You're going to hell, you fucking dyke bitch!" she yelled crazily at the gray-haired lady as the elevator doors closed.

The lady shrugged and became a little Indian girl. There came a knock at the door, and she went to answer it. "Hi!" she said, smiling widely.

"Hi, there!" answered an elderly black man, smiling back at her.

"Roger Pasternak, it is with pleasure that I announce to you that you are dead," the little girl said, a twinkle in her eyes.

"Hmmm, that explains a lot," Roger answered, a sudden look of worry in his eyes.

"What's wrong, Roger?" asked the little girl, reflecting his worried look.

"I'm an atheist. I don't believe in an afterlife."

"That's OK. I don't mind. I still believe in you, Roger!" the little girl said, smiling at him.

"You're God, aren't you?" the old man asked with sudden realization.

"Yup. A part of God, anyhow," the little girl said with a giggle.

"Hmmm..." Roger said, looking around him.

"So what do you want to do now?" asked the little girl.

"Well, what are my options?"

"Roger Pasternak, you have been, in your lifetime, a good and gentle man, an exemplary husband, an excellent father, a kindly neighbor and friend, and a pillar of your community. You resented no one, gave when you could, loved all, and tried to make your world and everyone else's a better place. You can now choose what you would like to do."

"Boy, you really don't make it easy, do you?" he said jokingly. "Truth is, I don't really *want* anything. I feel like I lived a good life, and that's all I wanted," he said seriously.

The girl extended her index finger and made a gesture that meant, "Come here." Roger got down on his knees, and the little girl cupped a hand to his ear. She whispered, "I love you!" and put her arms around the elderly man's shoulders and gave him a great big hug. The man let out a tear of pure joy and put his arms around the little girl, returning her love. When she let go, he felt as if he had been washed of all the pain he had suffered in his lifetime.

"I want to go back," he said.

The little girl smiled at him, took him by the hand, and walked him to the elevator. He saw himself in the mirror-like reflection of the metal and realized he was growing younger by the second. The little girl pressed the bottom button, and as Roger Pasternak entered the elevator, he was the same height and age as the young girl.

"I know you from when I was young!" he exclaimed.

"Yes," she said.

"Where does the top button lead to?" he asked, now a very young boy.

"The burning heart of the sun," replied God, smiling.

The baby in the elevator smiled back. "Goodbye."

The doors closed, and the elevator began its descent.

If you enjoyed these stories, please consider leaving a review on Goodreads.com or Amazon.ca.

58020456R00080

Made in the USA
Charleston, SC
01 July 2016